WHAT THE <u>REAL</u> CRITICS HAVE TO SAY

*I have always hated reading. Then I read your book
and now I understand why.*

– Flossie, aged 11, NSW

*I used to think Brussels sprouts were the most
disgusting thing in the world until I picked up one
of your books.*

– Elvis, aged 9.5, Victoria

*I laughed and laughed until I thought I would die.
Then I started reading your book.*

– Carmen, aged 10, Queensland

*I just couldn't put your story down. And when I
find my brother and his superglue I'm gonna kill him.*

– Everard, aged 96, Tasmania

*I believe your books are made from recycled
toilet paper. Seems a lot of trouble just to get back
to where you started.*

– Jonno, aged 5, WA

THE DOG THAT DUMPED ON MY DOONA

BARRY JONSBERG

ALLEN&UNWIN

First published in 2008

Allen & Unwin
83 Alexander Street
Crows Nest NSW 2065
Australia

Phone	(61 2) 8425 0100
Fax	(61 2) 9906 2218
Email	info@allenandunwin.com
Web	www.allenandunwin.com

National Library of Australia Cataloguing-in-Publication entry

Jonsberg, Barry, 1951-
The dog that dumped on my doona.

For primary school age.
ISBN: 978 174175 545 9 (pbk.)

A823.4

Designed by Bruno Herfst
Set in 10/14 pt Lino Letter by Midland Typesetters, Australia
Printed in Australia by Ligare Pty Ltd, Sydney Australia

This book is printed on FSC-certified paper.
The printer holds FSC chain of custody SGS-COC-004233.
The FSC promotes environmentally responsible,
socially beneficial and economically viable management
of the world's forests.

10 9 8 7 6 5 4 3 2 1

www.allenandunwin.com

For Gabrielle

I was woken up by a dog taking a dump on my doona.

It was really ugly.

Not the doona.

Not the dump, though that was pale, soft and curled like a meringue.

I mean the dog.

This dog was small and dirty-white and looked as if it had been pumping weights down at the local gym. It had a barrel of a chest and curved legs like you'd normally see on an old sideboard. An oblong head. Small, beady eyes.

We looked at each other.

I glanced down at the pile of poo steaming on my chest. So did the dog.

My first thought was that I was dreaming. I didn't even own a dog. The dog looked like it was dreaming too. It had a glazed expression all mixed up with deep satisfaction. A second or two ticked by.

'What the …!' I shouted, flinging back my doona and catapulting the poo into the corner of my bedroom where it landed and spread on the carpet with a soft thud. The dog sprang off the bed and glared up at me.

My bedroom window was open only a few centimetres. I found it hard to believe the mangy mutt could have squirmed through the gap.

'Shoo,' I said.

The dog didn't shoo.

'Go away,' I said, waving my arms about in a kind of go-away fashion.

The dog didn't do that either.

I sat on the edge of my bed and put my feet carefully on the floor. I was cold and scared. Even though the dog was small, it had attitude. And muscles. This was not a dog that other dogs would bully in a dog playground. This was a dog that other dogs would hand over their pocket money to. My mum often said that dogs wouldn't bother you, if you didn't bother them. Trouble is, this pooch seemed bothered by everything. Including my breathing.

I tried to hold my breath, but a low snarl told me that bothered him as well.

I stood up. Very, very carefully. *Now what?* I thought to myself. We could probably spend the rest of the night staring at each other, but I wasn't very excited by the idea. Or I could edge my way to the door, slip out and scream blue murder. Dad could come in and deal with the dog. That's what parents are paid for, after all.

I moved my right foot a few centimetres. The dog didn't

do anything. I brought my left foot over to the other. Still no reaction. Feeling encouraged, I did a quick scuttle round the end of the bed. He did the same. It was like he was tied to my legs with a short, invisible cord.

I was so scared that for a moment I thought the dog wouldn't be the only one dumping a loaf. I backed away into the corner. My heart was thumping in my chest. The dog moved slowly towards me. Stopped about a metre away. Looked up at me with hard, pink-rimmed eyes like marbles. Cocked his head to one side.

'Chill.'

The word was loud and clear. It seemed to fill the entire room. It even seemed to fill the inside of my brain. I jerked my head around. *Where did that sound come from?* There was no one lurking in the shadows of my room, yet I had heard the word as clear as day. I looked back at the dog. It hadn't shifted.

Then, with a speed that surprised me, it turned and jumped onto the window ledge, squeezed through the gap and was gone in a dirty-white flash. I started breathing again, the pumping of my heart loud in my ears. Suddenly I felt something wet and squishy under my bare feet. I looked down. A pale-brown mush was oozing through the gaps in my toes.

I'd stepped into something extremely nasty. And it was still warm.

Mum was not happy.

She made me take a shower while she cleaned up the mess on the carpet and changed my bedding. I'd hopped to her bedroom. One foot was covered with pale-brown poo and I didn't want to spread anything on the landing carpet. Trouble was, the hopping movement had splattered it all over the walls. Like those blood patterns you see in *CSI: Miami* or true murder TV programs.

She cleaned the walls too.

'Only you could do this, Marcus,' she said when I got back to my bedroom. 'Only you.'

'Mum, I didn't do it. The dog did.'

'Leaving the window open. Just asking for trouble.'

This struck me as unfair. Leaving a window open is not an invitation for anything outside to use your room as a Portaloo. But I kept my mouth shut. I get blamed for whatever goes wrong in this house. That's just the way it is. It's always all my fault. Eventually Mum finished making my bed and stomped off to her bedroom, and I snuggled down under the spare blanket.

It was so weird.

But weird things happen to me. They always have. I fell asleep and dreamed of a dirty-white dog with attitude and a bowel problem.

Dad was reading the newspaper when I made it into the kitchen for breakfast. Rose, my sister, sat opposite him. I poured cereal into a bowl, drowned it in milk and sprinkled in two large spoonfuls of sugar. Then I added another, just to be sure. Dad didn't glance at me as I took my seat.

'More protests in Queensland, it seems,' said Dad to no one in particular, head still bent over the paper.

'Really, Daddy?' said Rose. 'What about?' She smiled, flashing perfect teeth, and tilted her head to one side.

'Environmental groups are protesting about the building of more mineral mines out in the bush.'

'But why, Daddy?'

'They argue the minerals mined can only be used in the production of weapons and that therefore the money made is tainted. What's more, they point out that large areas of the bush are being destroyed and that there has been no research done on the effect on indigenous wildlife.'

Breakfast conversations are always this fascinating. Sometimes Dad talks about the stock exchange and I nearly poop my pants with excitement. So I concentrated on shovelling in cereal and tried to keep images of pooping out of my mind. I must have missed the next part of the conversation, because suddenly I realised I'd been asked a question.

'What?' I said.

Rose smiled at me.

'I was just asking you, Marcus, what you know about the butterfly effect.'

'It's an old movie.'

Rose laughed.

'No,' she said. 'I mean the idea that everything is connected, that you can't change one thing without it having an effect on something else. These mines. We don't know how they will change the environment. So, a butterfly flaps its wings in America and something changes in Australia.'

'It would have to be a humungous butterfly,' I argued. I got a mental picture of butterflies as big as skyscrapers, all beating their wings and knocking down New York City. I kept it to myself.

'You're so funny, Marcus,' chuckled Rose.

'Well,' said Dad, folding the newspaper, 'better get off to work.' As he left the kitchen, Rose gave a small wave.

'Bye Daddy,' she said. 'Have a lovely day.'

Last term, our class did a project on illusions – how some things are not really what they appear to be. I remember one picture our teacher showed us.

When I first saw it, I thought it was a young and pretty girl, her head turned away. But when I looked harder, I saw something else. An ugly old hag. The chin of the young girl became the nose of the old woman. Then it became a chin again. I guess the point is that the picture is both things at the same time. What you see depends upon how you look:

I looked at Rose.

The sun that had poured through the kitchen window while Dad was here disappeared behind a cloud. The temperature dropped like a brick. An icy chill ran down my spine and the hairs on my neck stood on end. Rose's face twisted. Her smile, which previously looked as if it was going to join up at the back of her skull and cause the top half of her head to drop off, was gone. Now her thin, bloodless lips were a pale gash on her face.

'You woke me up last night, Mucus,' she hissed. If she'd stuck her tongue out, I'd be willing to bet it would have been forked. I tried to answer, but *my* tongue felt like a lifeless slab. 'I need my sleep, you putrid little toad.'

'A dog dumped on my doona.' I forced the words out. 'Wasn't my fault.'

'It sure wasn't *my* fault, Mucus,' she snarled. 'And are

you certain you didn't just sneeze in the night and dump your brains onto the doona?' She laughed, a hideous cackle, at her own joke.

I sauntered towards the door. 'Up yours, Rose,' I said and legged it. I didn't stop running until I was halfway to school. I'd been here before. If Rose got hold of me, the bruises would take *forever* to fade.

Mum and Dad think the sun shines straight out of Rose's bum. Only I know that, beneath her sickly sweet exterior, beats a heart of pure evil.

The dog turned up when I was halfway to school.

One moment I was shuffling along, seriously considering the theory that Rose's body had been invaded by an alien life form. The next thing, I glanced to my left and it was there, trotting along and keeping pace. Still dirty-white, still the dog version of Arnold Schwarzenegger, but somehow not nearly as scary as it was last night.

I stopped. It stopped.

'Whaaaa!' I yelled, jumping up and down and waving my hands about. 'Graaah. Geddoutahere. Scram, ya mangy, scruffy piece of crap. Go on. Clear off.'

Look, I was angry, okay? This lump of filth had broken my sleep, got me into strife with Mum and Rose, and left a smell in my room that was starting to strip the paint off the walls.

The dog didn't so much as bat a pink eyelid. It looked up at me and cocked its head to one side. I could have sworn it was laughing.

'Oh, puhlease.'

The voice was all around. I leapt and did a quick three-sixty. There was no one there. No people. Not even any cars. I looked at the dog. It cocked its head to the other side. That was when I started to get scared again.

'That's right, bozo. Ya moron. Poop for brains. Great routine, by the way. Scary. I'm trembling in my boots. If I had boots, of course. Look, pal. Any more of that kind of nonsense and I'll rip your hamstrings out. You wouldn't like that. Plus, I'm fairly certain I've got rabies. Still, your choice, mate.'

So, I was standing in the middle of a deserted street, having a conversation with a dog. Well, not a conversation as such. More like a one-sided stream of insults. It was a warm day, but I came out in a cold sweat.

'I'm mad,' I said. It was a terrifying thought. I was going to end up like that old woman in the city centre who pushed a shopping cart around and sang religious songs to the pigeons. Or, even worse, like Mr Gaggins, the Assistant Principal at my school.

'You might be mad, matey. Probably are, come to think of it. I can see inside your head and it's a mess. But don't blame me. If you're crazy it happened a long time before I came along.'

I turned away and walked along the road. Head down. Eyes on the bitumen. *Don't think about it. Don't reply.* I might be bonkers, mad as a loon, one sausage short of a barbie, off my head, one oar in the water, but that didn't mean I had to give in to it. I *wasn't* going to give in to it. I'd get to school and feel better. Which would be a first.

'No point ignoring me, tosh,' said the dog.

Tosh?

'I'm on a mission from God,' it continued.

'*What*?' I stopped in my tracks. I couldn't help myself. 'A mission from God?'

The dog also stopped. It sniffed a tree and then cocked its leg. I watched while the steaming fountain seeped into the soil. The hound scratched itself behind the ear.

'That's what I said, mush. A mission from God. He needs your help.'

Mush?

'Let me get this right,' I said. 'I am having a conversation with a dog that crapped on my bedding in order to let me know that he has come from Heaven because God needs help from an eleven-year-old boy?'

'That's pretty much it, bucko.'

Bucko?

'Okay,' I said. 'I've got one or two problems with that. Firstly, this means you are a ghost dog, but what you did on my doona looked and smelled pretty real to me. Secondly, God – the all-powerful, all-seeing God, the dude who made the world and everything in it in seven days – doesn't send mangy canines on His business. No offence. The normal messenger, I believe, is an angel bathed in light with wings and a halo. Which you are not.'

'You *are* mad, aren't you?'

'Yes,' I said. 'Obviously. Barking mad. No offence this time either.' I started walking again. So did the dog.

'I know nothing about angels, with or without light, wings and a halo,' it said after about a hundred metres.

'I'm talking about the God in Pet's Heaven. The shop in the city centre mall.'

'God lives in a pet shop in the mall?'

'Last time I checked.'

Of course He does, I thought to myself. *Of course He does*.

I made it the last few hundred metres to the school gates in blissful silence. No voices in my head. No sound but traffic and the chatter of kids as they got out of cars and school buses. I kept my eyes fixed straight ahead of me. I even began to think that maybe the dog had gone, that if I looked down I'd see nothing. But when I turned in the school gates it was still there, sitting on the footpath. Those pink-rimmed eyes were fixed on me.

'We'll talk again,' said the voice in my head. 'That's a promise, my two-legged friend.'

I allowed myself to be swallowed in the rush of kids heading for the school building. It was official. I was off the planet. I was in orbit at the far reaches of the universe. One short step to singing to the pigeons. Me and the mall lady in a duet. The Space Cowboys. The Loons. The Singing Psychos.

If you want further proof, I was even looking forward to Maths. It was normal. Which is more than could be said for me.

'I'm mad,' I told Dylan at recess.

'Join the club,' he said.

Dylan is my best friend. But that was only one of the reasons I'd decided to let him in on the business of the talking dog. The main reason was that Dylan *is* mad. He's the first to admit it. And he has the pills to prove it. So I thought maybe he'd understand.

Okay. I guess it would depend on what you mean by insanity. But Dylan has been told by a whole bunch of experts that he had a behavioural disorder. I once asked him which one, ADD or ADHD? He said it was DAD: Dumb As Dogpoo. Which under the present circumstances was fitting, I suppose.

The thing is, Dylan isn't stupid. Not by a long shot. But he can't control what he says or what he does. Not really. Not fully. If it comes into his mind to say something – no matter how crazy – he'll just say it. He can't help himself. Same with doing mad stuff. If it strikes him as a good idea to stick his head down a toilet bowl he'll just go ahead and do it. I've seen it happen.

13

The real trouble is when something comes into Dylan's mind in classes. Like the time we were doing a science experiment involving electricity and he stuck a pair of scissors into a power point, blowing the mains and giving himself an afro which smoked at the ends. It took three teachers to stop him trying to repeat the effect once the electricity was back on.

So I figured that if there was one person in the whole world who'd listen to my story and take it seriously, it would be Dylan. Maybe he could suggest what tablets I could take. Not that he took the ones he was supposed to take. According to Dylan, they made him feel like a shadow.

'Wow,' he said when I'd finished. 'That is about the coolest thing I've ever heard. Can I meet him?'

'You don't get it, Dylan,' I said. 'It's not a real talking dog, ya moron. It's all in my head.'

'Yeah,' he said, reaching for his third can of cola that recess. Dylan doesn't eat, as far as I can tell. He just drinks cola. At any given moment he must be eighty per cent pure sugar. A teacher once told him to drink water and Dylan said he never drank water because fish pee in it. 'But what if, hey? What if? What if the dog *can* talk to you and it really *is* from God who does live in a pet shop because, after all, they say that God is everywhere and if He is everywhere then why can't He be in a pet shop as well as a church or in a meat pie or something and the big guy must be pretty busy all the time what with having, like, the whole universe to deal with so it might be right that He needs a bit of help from time to time, so He puts out feelers to find someone He can trust to do some of the small stuff while He concentrates on the big things like tidal waves and earthquakes and making new civilisations up in space which, let's be honest, must be a pretty big project and take up huge amounts of His spare time, so it's not impossible.'

Sometimes it's very tiring having a simple conversation with Dylan. Not that this was a simple conversation.

Dylan finished his cola and tossed the empty can over his shoulder. It hit the teacher on yard duty smack on the head. She had her back to us and the two hundred other kids who were sitting on benches around the canteen area. But, when she turned around, she was in no doubt about who'd done it.

'Dylan. Principal's office. Now!'

I was going to protest. How could she *know* it was Dylan, when there were hundreds of suspects all around? But I didn't get the chance.

'Good shot, eh, Miss?' said Dylan. It was clear he was pleased with himself. Sometimes he is his own worst enemy. Most of the time, actually.

The dog was still sitting on the footpath after school. In exactly the same spot.

'Is that it?' asked Dylan, all excited. Part of me was relieved he could see it as well. *But that proves nothing*, I thought. There's nothing unusual about a dog. It's a dog's ability to speak that makes it stand out from the crowd. And if it did speak, would Dylan hear it as well? I felt as if my entire mental health rested on what would

happen during the next few minutes. We walked over and stood next to the dog. The three of us gazed at each other for a few moments.

'Hello,' I said.

'What did it say, what did it say?' asked Dylan.

'Nothing, ya drongo,' I replied. 'Give it a chance, willya?'

But the dog didn't say anything at all. It stared, but there wasn't much interest there.

'Ugly piece of work, isn't it?' said Dylan after a while.

'Oi, ya twonk! Who you calling ugly? You should look in the mirror, mate.'

'Did you hear it? Did you …'

Twonk?

'… hear it?' I yelled.

Dylan looked blank.

'You didn't hear it, did you?' I said. He shook his head.

It was then that the dog gave a low growl. Dylan and I stared. The dog's hairs were standing up around his neck and it crouched slightly, in the promise of a spring. Its pink-rimmed eyes were fixed on Dylan, its loose lips curled back in a snarl. Slimy yellow teeth dripping with saliva were bared in a grim grin.

Dylan backed away a few paces. The dog followed, the growl getting deeper. The hairs on the back of *my* neck rose. If I'd had time to check out Dylan's neck I'm sure I would've seen that his had done the same. So, there were the three of us, all with hair standing to attention.

And then the dog leapt forward.

I have never seen Dylan move so quickly.

He was a blur.

Within point oh-one-six of a second, he had disappeared around a corner. And that must have been a hundred metres away. You could feel the air being sucked behind him. Branches of trees bent in the wind he made. The bitumen was smoking. Gone. *So much for friendship*, I thought. *Leave me to be chewed to a bloody pulp*, I thought. *Look after yourself*, I thought.

The dog hadn't budged from where it had landed. It sat on its dirty-white bum and scratched behind an ear. Its hairs had flattened.

'Got rid of that dropkick,' the voice in my head said. 'God is waiting, boyo.'

Boyo?

Look, I don't know how you'd behave, but at that moment I came to a decision. Maybe there was no point fighting against insanity. Maybe it was better to give in, go with the flow, enjoy the ride. Plus, I had a horrible feeling that it wouldn't be a good idea to keep God waiting.

'All right,' I said.

We went and sat in a deserted play area, me on a peeling bench and the dog laid out at my feet. Having given in to insanity, I decided I might as well try to be friendly, despite the poo on my doona.

'Shall I scratch your belly?' I said.

'Only if you want to lose your fingers,' said the dog.

So much for friendliness.

'Listen,' it continued. 'Shut your trap and pin back your

ears. I have important things to tell you and frankly I've got better things to do with my time than spend days chewing the fat with you.'

'Like what?' I asked. I was curious. What important things did dogs have to do?

'Chasing cats,' it said. 'Chewing up shoes, sniffing other dogs' bums. None of your damn business, mate. And I told you to shut up.'

I shut up.

'I'll make this quick,' it continued. 'You are a rare human being. So rare, in fact, that you are one in roughly five million people. Don't get superior about it, by the way. It's just an accident, all right? The way you were born. In every other respect, you are typically human. Below average intelligence, actually, which is a terrifying thing in its own right. But you were born with the ability to hear some animals, to communicate in a way that very few can. I am also unusual in that I can talk to you. Us animals are, of course, more intelligent and more highly developed than you, so the ability to communicate is limited to one in a million for us. The odds, therefore, against you ever being able to talk to an animal are ...'

'Big?' I said.

'Bigger than big.'

'Huge?'

'Huger than huge.'

'Colossal?'

'Let's not get bogged down in complicated statistical mathematics,' said the dog. 'Accept that our meeting is very, very unlikely. In fact, it couldn't have happened by chance. I have been searching for you. And now I've found you.'

'Because you are on a mission from God?'

'Exactly. And it is my job to pass that mission on to you. Any questions before we start?'

I did have one, actually.

'Did you fart?' I asked.

'Sure did.'

'It's foul.'

'You're lucky. My sense of smell is ten thousand times more sensitive than yours.'

There is nothing very interesting to see down a toilet bowl,
I thought, staring at the water gently rippling a few
centimetres from my eyes. It beat me why Dylan thought
it might be a fun thing to do.

'Say you're sorry and I won't flush,' said Rose.

It was all my fault. I should have been more careful.
But I was still thinking about the amazing story the dog
had told me and the incredible mission I'd been entrusted
with. So when I came home, I did what I always did.
Dropped my bag in the middle of the kitchen floor,
searched the fridge for something to eat and headed
straight for the toilet. I was just about to unzip when I
heard the door of the laundry cupboard open behind me.
There was no time to do anything. Rose jumped out,
grabbed me by the hair and stuffed my head straight
down into the bowl.

On the plus side, I hadn't had time to pee.

'C'mon Mucus,' she said. 'Say you're sorry.'

'Sorry,' I muttered.

21

'Can't hear you, Mucus!'

'Sorry,' I said as loud as I could.

'Sorry for what, Mucus? What are you sorry for?'

'For saying "Up yours" this morning. I am very, very sorry indeed.'

I know. Trust me, I know exactly how big a wuss I am. And I would dearly love to have been able to stand up for myself, maybe wrench my head from Rose's grip, twist around so that *she* was the one peering at lapping water and a couple of faint, disturbing stains on the porcelain. But she was just too strong. I put it down to alien genes.

Anyway, you'd reasonably expect that this cringing apology would do the trick. But you don't know my sister.

She flushed anyway.

This isn't finished, I thought as I dried my hair. *Not by a long chalk*. If Rose wanted a battle, she could have one. I could be patient. When you are faced with superior physical strength, you have to rely on cunning.

Dylan announced his presence by throwing stones at my bedroom window.

It would have been easier just to knock since we live in a single-storey house, but Dylan likes throwing stones. I opened the window and he slid into the room. This happens most afternoons. Mum has banned Dylan from the house. Ever since he wondered what would happen if you tried to dry a small pile of wet washing by stuffing it in our microwave for half an hour. The Fire Brigade didn't find it funny either.

'Wassup, Marc?' he said, slipping a can of cola from his back pocket and opening it. Jumping in through the window had shaken up the contents, so it fizzed all over the carpet. He rubbed the foam in with one dirty shoe and sipped the froth at the mouth of the can. 'What's that smell?' he added, wrinkling his nose.

'Blacky's calling card,' I said. 'The gift that keeps on giving.'

Dylan sat on my bed and started fishing for stuff in his nose. He does that a lot. Sometimes he mines so deep I worry his head is going to cave in.

'What you talking about, mate?'

'The dog. That's his name. Blacky. And the smell is what he left on my carpet last night.' Then I remembered the reason I was mad at Dylan. 'Oh, and thanks by the way.'

Dylan looked puzzled.

'For helping me out when the dog turned nasty,' I added. 'You know, throwing yourself in front of me, taking the full force of its attack just so I would be spared. You're a hero, mate. You should get a medal.'

Sarcasm goes straight over Dylan's head. Doesn't even ruffle his hair.

''s what friends are for,' he said.

Or maybe his short-term memory is so stuffed he simply can't remember.

'Dylan,' I said. 'I don't think I am going mad after all. I had a long talk with Blacky and he explained everything to me. It's weird, true. In fact, it's downright crazy, but I believe I *can* communicate with animals. Some, at least.

What's more, I have a duty to help someone in deep trouble. Blacky told me a sad story today. A really sad story. And I think we are the only people who can do anything about it. I say "we" because you *are* my mate and I know you will do anything for me.' *Apart from tackling a growling dog*, I added silently. 'What do you say?'

'Why's he called Blacky?' asked Dylan. 'When he's white. Sort of white, at least. More white than black, that's for sure.'

Maybe I'm old-fashioned. Or maybe I'm just normal. But if I had been told what I'd just told Dylan, I think my first question might have been slightly more … relevant, I suppose. I sighed.

'It's not his real name,' I said. 'He wouldn't tell me his real name. But Blacky is what he was called when he lived with a human for a while. He said the human called him that because he had this problem with his guts. The dog, I mean. So he was dropping smells all over the place and they were foul. And the human would yell at him and threaten him with a frying pan, so the dog would make a bolt for the door. That's when he called him Blacksmith, Blacky for short. Geddit? Made a bolt for the door? Blacksmith? Geddit?'

'No,' said Dylan.

'Never mind,' I said. 'The important thing is, will you help me?'

'What have we got to do?'

'Simple,' I said. 'We have to kidnap God.'

I couldn't get to sleep that night. It seemed to me that snatching God was something that was going to take planning and research. I was also hoping Blacky would show up but he didn't. That was a pity. I still had about ten million questions to ask him. And not just about the practical stuff that would help me fulfil my mission. He'd started me thinking about the bigger picture, the world and what we were doing to it.

For some reason, Rose's comment about the butterfly effect fluttered around in my head.

Saturday morning and it was raining.

This was no surprise, since on Saturday morning I play soccer for the local under-thirteens. I wasn't in the mood, partly because I was keen to get on with the God mission but mainly because I'm *never* in the mood. Dad, however, forces me. He was a goalkeeper when he was young, far back in the mists of time, and I think he likes to relive former glories through me.

Not that there is much glory involved in my play.

I am a hopeless goalkeeper.

It doesn't help that I am short for my age. It doesn't help that most of the other players are two years older than me and built like road trains. If they kick the ball just a little off the ground it goes over my head. The only reason I get picked for the team is that no one else wants to be goalkeeper.

There's a reason for that.

It's dangerous.

At every game you risk becoming eligible for the next Paralympics.

So I stood in front of the goal, soaking wet, taking up very little space and sizing up the opposition. They were big. And mean. You could see it in their eyes, which glowed red when the light struck them just right. Their very first attack was a one-on-one. A giant charged towards me. I could feel the ground shake. But I didn't have a choice. I had to advance, narrow down the angles. As it turned out I didn't get near him, which, to be honest, was a relief. It would have been like getting in the way of a tank. He belted the ball from about twenty metres and it fizzed past me into the roof of the net. Lucky I wasn't in the way. The net would have bulged twice. Once with the ball, once with my head.

As I picked the ball out, I noticed Blacky sitting by the touchline, looking amused.

'Your balance is all wrong,' he said. 'If you'd had your feet planted right, you could have got to that.'

'What?' I said. 'Now you're a football coach?'

'I am a student of the game,' he replied in this snotty voice.

I kicked the ball back towards the centre circle. *It isn't a good idea*, I thought, *to be seen talking to a dog on the sidelines*. It was this kind of behaviour that earned you the reputation of a fruitcake. I already had the reputation of a short goalkeeping disaster area and didn't need any others.

A soccer game lasts ninety minutes. This one seemed to take three days. Every time I picked the ball out of the net – which was often – Blacky would point out exactly where I went wrong.

'You are not dominating the area.'

The ball whizzed past my head again.

'You are not communicating with your defence.'

Bang. There went another one.

'Close in on the striker. That way, he has less room to get the ball past you.'

Yet another ball rocketed into the net.

'You're going to ground too early.'

By the twelfth goal, I'd had enough.

'Oi,' I said. 'Give it a break, willya? You are not helping me here.'

'You want help?' he said. 'I'll give you help, tosh.'

And he did. In the next attack the lumbering giant was through again and heading straight for me. It was like being in the path of a very large meteor. The guy was a human eclipse. And it was obvious he was going to take me out. Probably for good. I could see it in his eyes, so I closed mine and waited for the pain. But when the scream came, it wasn't mine.

I felt the ball bump gently against my ankles. When I opened my eyes I saw the big kid rolling around in agony. Not surprising, since he had a small, dirty-white dog attached to the front of his shorts. I winced. After that it was mayhem, with players, officials and fans (actually, my dad and a couple of other losers) trying to separate Blacky from the guy's groin. Blacky, in the meantime, was trying to separate the guy from his groin.

They had to abandon the game and call it a draw because the ref turned out to be the kid's dad and he had to take him to hospital. The other team wasn't pleased, especially as they were 12-0 up and it wasn't even half-time.

But officially, I had kept a clean sheet. First time and, I dare say, the last.

Blacky trotted up to me as I got my towel from the back of the goal.

'That's the way to tackle,' he said.

'You're suggesting I bite attackers in the you-know-where?'

He tilted his head to one side.

'Well,' he said. 'It certainly slows them down.'

One advantage of the game finishing early was that I could start on my mission earlier than expected. Dad had shopping to do in the town centre, so he left me outside the pet shop while he braved the crowds in the super-market. He'd be at least an hour, so I rang Dylan who lived fairly close. He said he'd get there in ten.

There was a bunch of people milling in the street, stopping passers-by and giving them leaflets. I picked one up when some guy just dropped it on the road after glancing at it. It was about the mineral mines in the Queensland bush. It asked people to write to the Premier, expressing their opposition. I folded the leaflet and put it in my pocket.

I examined the contents of the pet shop's windows while I waited for Dylan. I was waiting for Blacky as well. I'd been forced to leave him at the football ground. It was unlikely Dad would be thrilled to have the crotch-gnawing dog in the car with him.

It was the biggest pet shop in my town. It must have been one of the biggest in the state. I watched the kittens in their glass cabinets. Most were asleep in the sun's warmth – as soon as the soccer game had stopped, the clouds had cleared and the sun had broken through – but a few were climbing over each other and playing. There were dogs in the window too. And fish and snakes and other reptiles. It was like looking into Noah's Ark. So it seemed no time at all before I felt Dylan tug at my arm.

'Yo, Marc,' he said. 'The Dyl reporting for duty. What's happening?'

'This is a reconnoitre,' I replied.

'Excellent,' he said.

'You don't know what it means, do you?' I said.

'Nope.'

'We are checking things out, scoping the lie of the land, having a stake-out. Research, mate. Planning. Infiltrating enemy terrain.'

'Oh.'

Dylan sounded disappointed. He doesn't like looking at things. He's into action. Preferably involving lots of noise and plenty of stuff breaking. I couldn't find it in myself to tell him this mission was going to be boringly simple. I'd thought it over last night. All that about kidnapping God. I was overcomplicating the problem. The solution came to me in a blinding flash. Too easy.

We weren't going to kidnap God.

We were going to buy Him.

'Behold the face of God,' said Blacky.

I beheld it.

Kind of ugly, with a beard. Not long and white, but short, stumpy and grey. Big, lidless eyes set far apart. Leathery skin. The sign on the tank said PYGMY BEARDED DRAGON.

'And that's God, is it?' said Dylan, his face pressed up to the glass.

'Apparently,' I said.

'Not really what I was expecting,' said Dylan. 'Hey, look at him move! He went up that twig like lightning.'

'He's moving in mysterious ways,' I said.

That went pretty much over Dylan's head.

'So, what's the plan?' said Dylan. 'We've got to get the lizard out of the tank, right? Return him to his family in the wild, right? That's the mission the dog's set us, right?'

'Right,' I said. I'd already passed on the basics of what Blacky had told me. Not even Dylan could have failed to grasp them.

PET'S HEAVEN

'Okay,' said Dylan. 'I've got a plan. It's a good one, too. You and Blacky the white dog create a diversion. You go into the pet shop and ask them some tricky questions about terrapins or something. That'll be your job, Marc, 'cos dogs aren't real good at asking questions, even simple ones. So while you're distracting them … Better still, Blacky can chase a cat or something, knock over a few displays. That way, we've got two diversions – you and your terrapin questions, the dog wrecking the joint. Meantime, I put a brick through the window, grab the lizard and leg it. It's brilliant. It's simple.'

'Why am I not surprised that this fruitloop is your friend?' asked Blacky. I ignored him.

'I've got a simpler plan,' I told Dylan.

'What?'

'I go in and buy it.'

Dylan thought about this for a while.

'Yeah,' he said eventually. 'I admit it's simpler, but it's unbelievably boring.'

I had a hundred bucks saved up from my pocket money and birthday gifts from rellies who had no idea what eleven-year-old boys were into. The money was in a box under my bed. Dad had tried to convince me to put it in a savings account and I was glad I'd ignored him. I'd been saving for a hand-held games console, but that would have to wait. I wasn't thrilled by this, but what could I do? Turn my back on God?

It's weird. Everyone reckons Rose is a saint. And here I was giving up something I *really* wanted and no one would ever know. Life isn't fair, I guess. But then life certainly hadn't been fair to God.

I'd have explaining to do, true. Mum and Dad would want to know where the money had gone. I thought it unlikely they'd be thrilled to hear I'd spent it on a lizard. I could always tell them I'd bought God and that would be ten out of ten for cool. Unfortunately, it would also be zero out of ten for believability. Nonetheless, I was confident I could make up something.

Me and Dylan entered the shop. We left Blacky on the footpath. There was a sign on the door that said pets weren't allowed, which struck me as somewhat strange as well as destroying Dylan's brilliant plan. If the owner was being fair he'd have to move his entire stock outside onto the road. Anyway, I pointed my finger at Blacky's face.

'Sit,' I said. 'Stay. Good boy.'

'Talk to me like that again,' said Blacky, 'and you'll be minus an important part of your anatomy. I kid you not.'

'I'm trying to act like a responsible dog owner,' I hissed. 'Otherwise, someone might report you to the local council as a stray.'

He sighed inside my head, which is a very peculiar experience, believe me.

'All right,' he said. 'Just this once, though. I hate all that macho, man's-best-friend garbage. It's demeaning. And don't you *ever* ask me to play dead, shake your hand or roll over. I know where you live, remember?'

But he did sit. Reluctantly. Dylan and I pushed open

the door of the pet shop but before we got in, I could hear words ringing in my ears.

'Fetch,' said Blacky in my head. 'Good boy.'

I really disliked that dog's attitude. Particularly since I was the one doing him a favour.

'*How* much?'

I nearly yelled it. Surely he couldn't be serious?

'Two hundred and sixty dollars. It's a pygmy bearded dragon, you know. Quite expensive.'

'At that price, you'd expect it to be a fully grown bearded dragon,' I pointed out.

The guy behind the counter chuckled. He was short and bald with a long bushy beard. It was like someone had put his head on upside down. If he could breathe fire, he'd be a pygmy bearded dragon himself.

'You don't know much about reptiles, do you?' he said. 'Bearded dragons are not generally expensive. You can get them for about sixty bucks, normally. But the pygmy is the most expensive of the lot. And this specimen has rare markings which puts the price up even more. You won't find one like this cheaper anywhere.'

'I haven't got that kind of money,' I said.

'Do you have a tank to keep it in?' he asked. I shook my head.

'Ah,' he said. 'Then you are talking about equipment, lighting, heating as well. You'll have to add on another five or six hundred bucks for all that. If you want that pygmy and you want it to stay alive, then you're talking the best part of a thousand dollars.'

A *thousand* dollars?

'If that's too much, we have a bearded dragon that's only sixty. Good pets, they are.'

'It has to be that one.'

'Then you'd better save your pennies, kid,' he said. He was remarkably cheerful talking about how expensive everything was. It was like I had made his day by not being able to afford to buy God from him.

'Don't sell him,' I said as I headed for the door. 'I'll be back.'

His beard parted and some noise came out, but I didn't hear what it was. With that level of soundproofing around his mouth, it wasn't surprising.

Back on the footpath, I did some quick maths. I was a hundred and sixty bucks short. Forget about all that equipment. That wasn't going to be necessary. But a hundred and sixty bucks? That was a fortune.

Blacky studied me. He didn't have to ask the question. It was in his eyes.

'This isn't going to be as simple as I thought,' I said. 'God costs a lot more than you'd expect.'

'Just so you know,' said Blacky. 'Time is short. You have only five days. So I respectfully suggest, mush, you get your skates on.'

I failed to spot the respect in his voice, but I didn't dwell on it. You see, a dim light had pinged on above my head.

'There's still my brick idea,' said Dylan hopefully. His fingers clenched and unclenched. You could tell he was itching for some destructive action.

'Hold the brick,' I said. 'No. I don't mean hold the brick. I mean, we'll keep that plan on the back burner. I've got another idea.'

'Better make it quick,' said Blacky.

I was really starting to hate that dog. I hadn't liked him to begin with. I was doing my best here, willing to spend all my savings. And for what? Nothing that was going to help me, that was for sure. I didn't stand to gain anything. But this hound wasn't in the slightest bit grateful. I hadn't asked for this job and there was no way I was going to be made to feel guilty just because I couldn't do it immediately.

'Look,' I said. 'Clear off, the pair of you. I need to do some thinking. Come and see me tonight. Hopefully, I'll have something to report.'

'Okay,' said Dylan. 'I'll use the time to improve my brick-throwing skills.'

Someone was in for a disturbing afternoon. It was comforting to know I wasn't going to be the only one.

'*How* much?'

I nearly yelled it. Surely he couldn't be serious?

This felt like déjà vu.

'Thirty bucks,' he said. 'That's it. Not a cent more.'

I put the phone against my chest and tried to keep calm. When I was sure I wasn't going to lose it big time I got back on the line.

'It's worth ten times that and you know it, David,' I said. 'You chiselling cheapskate chunk of snot.' Well, okay. I didn't say that last bit. Never let it be said I don't know how to conduct delicate negotiations. 'It's hardly been used,' I continued. 'And it's a bargain at a hundred and sixty.'

'It's even more of a bargain at thirty,' he said.

It was clear that David wasn't quite so delicate in his bargaining skills.

'That's true, mate,' I said. 'But you are forgetting one thing. I won't sell it to you for thirty. I would sooner give it the Salvos than let you have it for that price. I would sooner smash it into pieces with a hammer and then set fire to it than let you get your fingers on it for thirty. One hundred and twenty. That's the lowest I can go. And it's still robbing me blind.'

I looked down at the iPod on my bedside cabinet. I wasn't exaggerating. This thing was top quality. Eighty gig, black, video. Top of the range.

'Thirty-two,' he said.

I sighed. The thing is, I knew David was loaded. He has parents who own BMWs. Not one. Two. Plus they go on overseas holidays about five times a year. He could afford to buy a new iPod like mine. But maybe that's how rich people become rich – by never spending more than they have to. Ever since I'd taken my iPod to school, he'd wanted it. In fact, David had bugged me about selling it to him, even though I'd only had it for the week since my birthday.

'Thirty-two dollars, fifty cents,' he said.

'Bye, David,' I said.

'Thirty-three,' he said.

'You know my number,' I said and hung up.

I was in a black mood. Not because David wasn't going to buy it. But because there was only one other person who wanted to buy the iPod from me and could afford it. Trouble was, I didn't think I could bring myself to do it. I almost came out in a cold sweat just thinking about it. In fact, I knew that if I did think about it anymore, it would never happen. So I picked up the iPod, walked down the corridor and knocked on her door. I tried to keep my mind blank.

'Is that you, Mummy?' called Rose. Her tone of voice was so sweet it was probably rotting her teeth.

'No. It's me. Marcus.'

'Well, don't just stand out there, Mucus,' she said. 'Clear off.' The sweetness had been replaced by acid. I was surprised the paint on her bedroom door didn't blister.

'Rose. I need to talk to you.' I tried to keep *my* voice calm and reasonable.

'So write me a letter.'

'Please?' God, I hated myself. I was going to sell her my iPod and here I was pleading with her to rob me.

The silence behind her door was deafening.

'I want to sell you my iPod,' I said to the big sticker she has on her door. *If It's Too Loud, You're Too Old*. What a loser. The sticker disappeared and Rose's face appeared instead. Normally, where I'm concerned, Rose moves at a slug's pace. I could be drowning and she'd finish texting her friends before dialling ooo. If she could be bothered. Now she'd nearly pulled a muscle getting to the door. 'Come in,' she said.

I counted the money twice, but it still didn't come to more than a hundred.

I won't go over all the details of my negotiations with Rose. It's too painful. Suffice it to say that in the end she bargained me down by pointing out that buying the iPod was going to be a risky business. Mum and Dad had only bought it for me the previous week. There was a danger, she said, that they would insist on her returning it if they found out she'd bought my only birthday present.

Though I hate to admit that Rose *ever* talks sense, she had a point. So I swore to secrecy. I also swore that I would say I had lent it to her if questions were asked. I had to pay the price for this inconvenience. She cut twenty bucks off the asking price on the grounds she couldn't declare the iPod was officially hers. I mean, Rose wasn't bothered about robbing me. She'd have ripped me off, poked out my eyes and sold me to white slave-traders in a flash if she could. It was only the *practical* side of robbing me that bothered her.

It's no real surprise I wouldn't urinate on her if she was on fire.

I tried to block out all thoughts of my sister as I did the maths.

Still sixty bucks short.

And time was running out.

The phone rang.

'Okay, then,' said David. 'You win. I'll give you a hundred and sixty.'

It was like someone had smacked me around the face. I'd told him – not ten minutes before – I'd take a hundred and twenty. He offered thirty-three. Then he jumped in with this bid. Was it just me or was the whole world going crazy?

I thought about Rose in her bedroom, plugged into my iPod. I thought of her reaction if I went back in there and offered to refund the cash.

I put the phone down carefully. I didn't want David to hear me sobbing.

'I'm not sure I've got any jobs you can do,' said Mum, pulling sheets out of the washing machine.

'I could put those on the line for you,' I suggested.

'That's very kind of you, dear,' she said, bundling the soggy mass into my arms.

'How much?'

'Sorry?'

'For putting the washing on the line.'

'Are you serious, Marcus?' she replied. She had this hurt look on her face. 'You want to be paid for that? A small job that will take you about two minutes? When I feed you, wash your clothes, tidy your room, buy you clothes...'

I hung the washing on the line and tried Dad.

'You could mow the lawn,' he said.

'How much?'

'All of it.'

It wasn't worth arguing. I mowed the lawn. Excellent. Two boring jobs. No money. This wasn't going to work. I darted across the road to number forty-three. It was time to get serious.

Mrs Bird lived up to her name.

She was tiny and had a hooked nose like a beak. She also put her head to one side when she talked. Every time I spoke to her I had an urge to offer her a handful of seeds just to see if she'd peck at them. Mrs Bird was also ancient. I'd seen pictures of Egyptian mummies that looked younger. She'd lived on her own at number forty-three since her husband had died back in about 1952. As far as anyone could tell, she had no relatives. Probably outlived them all. So the neighbourhood kept an eye on her. There was no roster or anything. People just knocked on her door from time to time to see if she wanted any jobs done or if she needed anything from the shops.

But mainly to see if she was still alive.

Mrs Bird had a cat with a serious weight problem, due to the fact that she shovelled food down its throat from morning to night. She'd turned it into a hairy beach ball on legs. Not that you could *see* its legs beneath the rolling mounds of blubber. When it stopped, its stomach wobbled on for another two or three minutes.

I had a theory. Beneath the cat's obese exterior a slim and supple beast was trying to get out. Given its size, maybe two or three slim and supple beasts. I had visions of before-and-after photographs. One looking like a tortoiseshell cow-pat, the other on a beach with a six-pack and a bikini. Okay, I'm exaggerating. But I reckoned someone should care about the strain being placed on the cat's heart by its unnatural girth.

Maybe Mrs Bird felt that way occasionally, because she had been known to pay to have the cat exercised.

I knocked on the door and waited for her to answer. This took ten minutes. Like her cat, Mrs Bird was not known for quick or sudden movements. Finally though, the door creaked open and her face appeared, her hooked nose like a blade arcing towards me from a nest of wrinkles. She smiled and the wrinkles writhed like something insane.

'Hello, Sonny,' she said. She called everyone Sonny. Maybe because she was so old, it was the only name she could keep in her head.

'Hello, Mrs Bird,' I said. 'I wondered if you'd like me to take Tiggles for a walk.' That was the cat's name. Tiggles.

'I think I might be short of cornflakes,' said Mrs Bird.

That was the other thing about Mrs Bird. Short. Birdlike. And stone-deaf. It took me another five minutes to make her understand what I meant.

'That is very kind of you, Sonny,' she said. 'I will pay you, of course.'

'Only if you insist, Mrs Bird,' I replied.

'About half-past eleven,' she said.

I sighed. You couldn't afford to worry too much about time when you were having a conversation with Mrs Bird.

I snapped the lead to the front frame of the treadmill in our garage, keeping my fingers well away from Tiggles. It couldn't waddle two paces if you put a fresh salmon in front of it, but if your flesh was within striking distance of its paws it'd lash out at the speed of light.

I had a theory about that as well. I reckoned that its size made it unhappy and depressed. It couldn't be easy being a slim and supple beast trapped inside the body of a walrus. I'd lash out as well.

Once the mog was secure I plugged in the treadmill and put the machine on a programmed incline. When I pressed the start button, the cat moved down the belt until the lead started to choke it.

I had done this before. It was an idea born out of desperation. The first couple of times I had walked it, the cat didn't move. Went limp and unresisting. I hadn't taken it for a walk. I'd taken it for a drag. The animal was so heavy it was like dragging a furry cannonball along the street. I ran out of energy while Tiggles didn't use any at all. This was not the idea.

Then I remembered the treadmill in our garage. It was never used. When I first stuck the cat on the moving treadmill, it just slid down the belt and got dumped on the floor. I had worked on the idea it wouldn't like ending up as a splat on the tiles, but I hadn't realised how stubborn it was when it came to exercise.

So I kept it attached to the lead. Now it had a choice. Walk or die of strangulation.

I know what you're thinking. This is cruel. This is nasty. Normally, I'd agree.

But wouldn't it be more cruel to allow it to slowly inflate like a cat-shaped balloon? At some point it would explode and I didn't want to be around when that happened. The mess would be spread around the entire neighbourhood. Buildings within the blast radius could be destroyed. No. Enforced exercise was better than no exercise at all. The way I looked at it, I was saving its life.

I didn't give Tiggles more than half an hour. I was worried its heart would give out. When I switched the machine off it slumped down on the mat into what looked like a coma. But I was prepared for this as well. I got a large shovel under it and, using all my strength, levered it onto my ancient skateboard. Then I wheeled it back to Mrs Bird's house.

'Thank you so much, Sonny,' she said as I tipped the flabby feline onto her living room floor. It still didn't move, unless you counted its belly spreading out over two square metres of the carpet. 'I'll get my purse.'

No one knew whether Mrs Bird had any money or not. Some of the kids who lived nearby reckoned she was a multi-millionaire who kept it all stashed underneath her mattress. But no one knew for sure.

And she was so tiny. And wrinkled. And old.

When she came back and held out a twenty-dollar note to me, I was caught in two minds. This would reduce the amount I would have to find to forty dollars. This was manageable. I could see light at the end of the tunnel. Hey, given that Mrs Bird was so forgetful, I could come back in five minutes and do it all over again. And again. Half an hour and I'd have the cash to buy God.

But she was so tiny. And wrinkled. And old.

'That's okay, Mrs Bird,' I said. I couldn't stop the words coming out of my mouth. I tried. 'It's my pleasure. I don't need payment.'

I have to be honest here. I'd walked that cat dozens of times and never been paid for it. I always meant to take the cash she offered, but when it came down to it my fingers couldn't grasp the money. I'm pathetic.

'Are you sure?' she said, tucking the note back into her purse.

I'd noticed that about Mrs Bird before. Sometimes she heard things as clear as a bell. I guess her hearing just came and went.

'Absolutely, Mrs Bird,' I replied. 'I enjoy it. Really. No charge.'

'You're right,' she said. 'It *is* a lovely day.'

It must have gone again.

I would have sighed but I screamed instead. I'd taken a step backwards and put my foot too close to Tiggles's dozing mass. It had lashed out with razor-sharp claws and taken a chunk out of the flesh at my ankle. Payback time.

I limped back to my house, trailing a thin stream of blood.

Three jobs, a gash that would probably get infected and no money to show for any of it. I thought I would just lie on my bed and listen to music on my iPod. It had been a helluva day. Then I remembered what had happened to my iPod and my mood just got darker.

'You poop on my doona again and the deal's off,' I said.

I meant it too. I was sick of the whole business.

Blacky lay at the foot of my bed. I'd tried to stop him but he took no notice. Dylan lay at the top end of my bed. I'd tried to stop him, too, but he didn't pay attention to me either. Sometimes, I just felt it was so unfair that everyone took Marcus for granted. Now I was on the point of exploding. So I stood at the open bedroom window and looked at the night stars. That calmed me sometimes. Helped me see that my problems were pretty small compared to everything out there.

'Chill, man,' said Blacky. 'I did that just once to get your attention. Won't happen again.'

I snorted.

'Is he talking to you again?' asked Dylan.

'Look. Just shut up,' I said. 'I can't have two conversations at once.'

'Fair enough,' said Dylan. 'I can't even cope with one.'

He whipped out a hand-held computer console and

started loading up a game. I sat on a chair and looked at Blacky's curled-up body. When I spoke again I kept the words in my head.

'I'm not sure I can do this,' I said.

'Sure you can,' said Blacky. 'It's not difficult. Even someone with your limited intelligence should be able to cope with a simple problem-solving exercise like this.'

'Hey,' I yelled. It was strange yelling and not making a sound. 'Why are you so horrible to me? I haven't done anything to you. In fact, despite what you've done to me, the dump, the threats, the nastiness, the disgusting smells, I've tried to do what you asked. I've sold my iPod, I've been scratched, I've undergone humiliation. And all for what? So I can spend two hundred and sixty dollars on a wretched reptile that will then be released into the wild. What do I get out of it, huh? Zilch. Zip. Nothing.'

Blacky didn't react to anything I said. He just flicked an ear.

'So maybe you should just be a bit nicer to me,' I continued. 'If you think I'm such an idiot, why don't you do this job yourself, eh?'

'I'll give you the answer in two words,' said Blacky. 'Opposable thumbs.'

'What?'

'Opposable thumbs. The only reason you humans are so successful. Just an accident of evolution, but it means you can manipulate things, make tools, change the environment. Boy, have you changed the environment!'

'Oh yeah?' I said. I wasn't going to let this go. 'And what

about intelligence, huh? Our ability to think, imagine, create? No other living things can do what we can do.'

The dog licked his testicles. I didn't know if this was a comment on what I was saying, but I waited patiently. Eventually, he uncoiled himself.

'You are absolutely right,' he said finally. 'Humans are unique. I cannot argue with you when you say that no other living thing would do what you guys do.'

I smiled.

'Global warming,' he continued. 'Environmental change, destruction of habitats. Humanity is in a league of its own.'

'But ...'

'Shut up,' snarled Blacky. 'Shut up and listen while I give you a few facts. You might learn something. Did you know that ten years ago, thirty thousand species a year were becoming extinct? That's three every hour. Gone. Never to come back. And since then it's all got much worse. Since you have been born, tosh, a minimum of three hundred thousand species have disappeared. And all because of humankind and what it is doing to this planet. Just take global warming – by itself. That will result in *a further million* species becoming extinct in the next thirty years. With all the other changes that humankind is bringing about, Earth will lose at least a third of all species, possibly up to seventy per cent, by 2050. Animals, plant life, insects. Wiped out. That's what your intelligence is doing, mate. The greatest extinction event in the history of the planet. You should be proud.'

I spluttered.

'That's … that's just not true. You're making it up. I mean, I know we are damaging the earth, but…'

'Those aren't my figures, mush. They come straight from your scientists. Look it up.'

That was unbelievable. Simply unbelievable. Suddenly, the dog had gone. I caught a glimpse of a dirty-white shape flickering at the corners of my vision. Then nothing. I stared out of the window. The night was clear. I could hear cicadas chirping and somewhere, far off, the rumble of a tree frog. Suddenly I felt tired.

'Hey, man,' said Dylan. 'Tell the story. Go on, Marc. Tell us the story.'

'What story?' I said, but my voice was weak even to my own ears.

'The story of God the bearded dragon. Why he is so deep in the brown stuff and why we have to rescue him. Come on, man. You promised.'

I had promised. But I wasn't in the mood right now.

'Too tired, Dylan,' I said. 'Tell you tomorrow at school, mate. I swear.'

'You'd better,' he muttered.

It still took twenty minutes to get him to leave. As soon as he'd gone I went along to the living room. Mum and Dad were watching TV.

'Dad?' I said. 'Can I use the internet for about half an hour?'

We only have one computer in our house and its use is strictly rationed. Mum and Dad reckon that left to my own devices I'd just be playing games all the time. This is amazingly unfair and, at the same time, amazingly true.

So I have to book time on it when I need to do homework.

'Schoolwork?' asked Mum.

'A project on mankind's effect on the environment,' I said.

As it turned out, I didn't need the full half-hour. The information was there, just like Blacky said it would be. What made the reading even more depressing was that I came to understand the dog was not exaggerating.

If anything, the full picture was even worse than he claimed.

I couldn't sleep.

At about two in the morning I got up and opened the window wide. For once, the night air was mild and I breathed it deep into my lungs. Summer was on its way. I don't know why, but I got the urge to get out of the house. I wanted to feel the grass under my toes. Maybe lie on my back and watch the stars. So I swung my legs over the windowsill and dropped to the ground. I listened but there was no sound from Mum and Dad's bedroom. They'd kill me if they knew I was out at that time of night.

I lay on my back. The stars were hard pinpricks through black material. They crowded the sky. I could hear small night noises, the gentle swoosh of wind through leaves, the faint scurrying of insects and small animals moving through their worlds. It was so peaceful out there.

But not inside my head.

I wanted to shout, to scream.

Not an option.

So I gathered my concentration and yelled as hard as I could inside my mind. My head rang with it.

'It's not my fault,' I howled. 'I'm just a kid. I didn't do any of that. It's not my fault.'

The night did not reply.

'What can I do?' I asked. I wasn't expecting an answer, but when it came it was in a voice I recognised. I jerked my head up but there was no sign of Blacky anywhere. Just the glow of the streetlight and the darkness trying to press it back.

'Do what you can,' said the voice in my head. 'And start by telling people. As many as possible.'

I sat up, cross-legged. The dampness from the ground was soaking through my pyjama bottoms, but I barely noticed.

'You cannot change everything by yourself,' the voice continued. 'But you *can* do the small stuff. Spread the word. And protect. One animal at a time, tosh. One animal at a time.'

Then the voice was gone and I knew somehow it wouldn't return that night.

I slipped back into my bedroom and found the leaflet in the pocket of my shorts. The leaflet I'd picked up from the street. I read it again by the light of the torch I kept for late-night reading beneath my doona. Then I wrote a letter to the Premier on a page ripped from an old exercise book. It wasn't a long letter. The leaflet suggested I keep it short and businesslike. I sealed it in an envelope and placed it on my bedside table.

Finally, I turned off the torch, put it under the bed and crawled under the doona. I felt full of energy and purpose. My blood was racing and I doubted I would sleep at all. But I soon felt sleep folding over me. My last thought was of something I had read somewhere. Or maybe it was something I had been told once. It didn't really matter.

An avalanche, I remembered, could start by the small shifting of one individual snowflake.

There was just me, Dad and Rose at breakfast. I started with Rose.

'Take gorillas,' I said. 'The destruction of rainforests in Africa is threatening their habitats. Unless we're very careful, they could be extinct before we know it.'

Rose filled her cereal bowl and brought it to the kitchen table. As she passed, she whispered in my ear.

'I wish *you* were extinct, Mucus.'

She put her bowl down and flashed brilliantly white teeth around the table as she sat.

'It is sooo wonderful you are taking an interest in the environment, Marcus,' she trilled. 'Daddy? Don't you think so?'

Dad nodded and smiled. At Rose, not at me. That's the problem with dealing with Rose. She has built up such a reputation for angelic behaviour that no one would believe me if I spilled the beans on her true nature. It would be like accusing Snow White of being a shoplifter. Nonetheless, I thought I could use the situation to my advantage.

'That's great,' I said, whipping out the rather crumpled leaflet and placing it in the centre of the table. 'Then maybe you guys would like to write a letter protesting about the Queensland mines. I have.' I waved my envelope around. 'We need to make a stand. For the future of the planet.'

Rose's eyes narrowed, but I reckon Dad missed it. Maybe she thought I was trying to steal her halo, replace her as the golden child of the family. She needn't have worried. I couldn't compete. I didn't want to compete.

Dad picked up the leaflet and glanced through it.

'I'll give it some thought, Marcus,' he said. 'I admire your principles, but there are other things here to take into consideration. The benefits to the economy, for example, are huge and there is no real evidence that wildlife has been affected in the slightest.'

I knew better. Trouble was, I couldn't tell anyone God's story as Blacky had related it to me. Who would believe it?

But it wasn't often that Dad gave me any praise at all, so I thought this might be an opportunity.

'Dad?' I said. 'Can I have sixty bucks to buy a pygmy bearded dragon from the pet shop in the mall?'

'When hell freezes over,' he replied, returning to his newspaper.

Rose sneered at me while Dad's head was buried in the pages. Then she put her right hand to her forehead in the loser sign. I was thrilled to see she had forgotten to put her spoon down and that a big dollop of Weet-Bix fell onto her clean white school shirt. She shrieked, jumped and splattered more of her cereal over a wide area, including the bald spot on Dad's head.

'Oh, Daddy!' she shrieked. 'I am sooo sorry. I'm sure Marcus didn't mean to jog my arm. Here. Let me clean up this mess.'

She bustled around the kitchen, finding paper towels, and then mopped up the pale sludge from Dad's head. I picked up my school bag and headed for the door. I couldn't help it. I turned back and grinned. After all, it wasn't often Rose let her halo slip. She met my eyes over Dad's shoulder. I knew trouble when I saw it.

'That's all right, petal,' said Dad. 'Just a small accident. No harm done.'

Not yet, I thought.

But I'd worry about it later. Right now, I had plenty on my plate. Postbox, school and a pressing economic problem ...

'We need sixty bucks,' I told Dylan at lunchtime. 'And time is running out.'

'No worries,' he said, popping open his third can of cola. 'Why?'

It was frustrating talking to Dylan. He forgot everything so quickly. To be honest, it was a minor miracle that he remembered who he was most days.

'Dyl, ya dill,' I said. 'The bearded dragon, remember? Two hundred and sixty bucks, of which I have two hundred. Two sixty minus two hundred equals ... what?'

Dylan gave the matter some thought.

'A problem,' he said.

'Correct,' I said. Maths has never been Dylan's strong point. Ask him how many toes he's got, give him specific directions, including a mud map and a calculator, and he's still liable to be off by at least fifteen. 'And here's another problem for you. How do we raise sixty bucks? Quickly.'

'That's easy,' he said.

'Oh yeah?' I said. 'How?'

'I'll get you sixty bucks by first thing tomorrow morning. On one condition.'

'What?'

'You tell me the story of God the bearded dragon.'

He hadn't forgotten that. We *are* surrounded by minor miracles. Trouble is, I needed a fairly large one. But fair's fair. I *had* promised to tell him. So, while Dylan slurped his cola and explored the deepest parts of his nose for interesting specimens, I started.

O**NCE** upon a time, there was a bearded dragon who lived in the Queensland desert. His name was God. That wasn't his real name, of course. But no one other than another bearded dragon could pronounce his real name. So that will have to do.

And, in many ways, God is a good name because he ruled over all his world. A small world, true, by human standards. Just a patch of desert. Sometimes another bearded dragon would try to muscle in on that world. Normally a young dragon trying to impress. But God was too strong.

He'd just puff out his beard, which was longer and more bristly than any other rival's, and frighten them off. Not much changed in God's world and that was okay by him. He was a happy dragon. Food was in good supply. His eight wives were all happy too. They raised a family. A large family.

No. God didn't like change. But that didn't mean change couldn't come. And that it couldn't come in small ways, ways he wasn't able to see.

Not far from where he lived there was a mine. A mineral mine. Hundreds of people worked there. But God didn't really care. As long as the people didn't bother him, he was fine. And they didn't mean to bother him. It was just that they needed somewhere to put the waste from their mine. It was an accident that the place they chose was also God's world. It was also an accident that what they put there was poison. Not to people, true. But to bearded dragons.

God didn't know his world was going to die until he felt the changes in his body. Most were deep within, but there was also another change. His skin changed colour. Became lighter. Mottled. And that was very unlucky because a light, mottled skin makes bearded dragons more valuable to those who collect them.

As chance would have it, a worker at the mine – the worker who caught God – was a reptile enthusiast. He knew that God could make him fifty dollars. He knew a breeder in the city who was on the lookout for new dragons. Reptile breeders are bound by strict laws. Taking animals from the wild is not allowed. There are harsh penalties for anyone doing so if they are caught by rangers from Parks and Wildlife.

But it is a big desert and there aren't many rangers. Not many at all.

God was taken to the city and the breeder paid good money for him. He was going to use him for breeding, but then he noticed the dragon was sick. It was too late to get his money back, so he sold him on. To a pet shop. He could do that. He was a registered breeder and the paperwork couldn't really be checked.

So God finds himself alone in a tank, in a window, dying. He doesn't care so much about himself. He has had a good life. But he cares about his family and his poisoned world. He needs to get back and warn his family. Move them. Maybe it is too late. Probably is for most. But some of his family might survive. If he can warn them. So he tells his story to a small and rather ugly dog that stops outside the pet shop one day. The dog promises he will help.

But time is running out. It is running out quickly.

'That's sad,' said Dylan.

'Yeah,' I said. 'Which is why we need that sixty bucks.'

Dylan finished what was in his can and then looked down the ring-pull opening as if hoping the can would magically refill itself.

'I'll have the money for you tomorrow morning,' he said. 'I already told you that.'

'Yeah, but how, Dylan?' I know Dylan and his family. They have no money to speak of. Church mice are rich by comparison.

'Hey, man,' replied Dylan, tapping his finger against the side of his nose. 'That's for me to know and you to find out. But it's in the bag, mate. In the bag. Good as gold. I have a cunning plan.'

I sighed. Dylan's cunning plans normally involve rocks, huge amounts of stupidity and the breaking of glass and laws alike. I was glad he was keeping it to himself.

'Can I have a closer look at the bearded dragon, please?' I asked the guy in the pet shop.

It wasn't the man with the polished head and the beard you could hide a ride-on mower in. This guy was young, enthusiastic and full of energy.

'No worries, mate,' he said.

He skipped over to the tank. I followed. We pressed our faces up against it. The guy tapped lightly on the glass. 'He's a beauty, isn't he?'

'Yeah,' I said. There was a long pause. 'So you reckon I could get a closer look?'

The guy frowned.

'Not sure we can get much closer,' he said.

'I mean, could you get him out of the tank?' I asked. 'Put him on your hand, or something?'

He frowned again.

'Aw, mate,' he said. 'Not sure about that. They can be pretty vicious, you know. I knew someone who tried to handle a bearded dragon. Lost his little finger. Not worth the risk, mate. I'm attached to my fingers.'

'The other guy said they make great pets,' I pointed out.

'Mate, they do. They make terrific pets.'

'Even if they're vicious?'

The guy mulled this over for a while. He frowned and smiled at the same time, which was peculiar to watch.

'You want the truth, mate? I have no idea if they're vicious or not. Truth is, I not only know nothing about animals, I'm scared of them. I was once savaged by a budgie.'

'So losing a finger to a psycho bearded dragon? That was a lie, then?'

He grinned.

'I make it up as I go along, mate. I'm what you call eccentric, but harmless.'

I let him return to the desk. There didn't seem much point in continuing the conversation. I shuffled round the side of the tank and peered in. There was a tangle of branches in there, as well as a number of fair-sized rocks. I couldn't see the bearded dragon.

I glanced around the shop. At least it was empty of customers. I'd have felt very strange talking to an apparently empty glass tank with an audience.

'Hey, God,' I whispered. 'I'm doing my best, man. Sorry, dragon. But I've got problems raising the money. Listen, I haven't given up, that's all I'm saying. And, one way or another, I'm going to get you out of there. I swear. Even if we have to go with Dylan's plan involving distractions, bricks and a ram raid. So just hang on, okay, God. Have faith.'

There are times when you just know someone is behind you. Close behind you. This was one of those times. I turned my head and the pet shop guy was right there, just behind my right shoulder. He was looking at the tank and grinning.

'I'm talking to God,' I said as calmly as I could. 'This is a private matter between me and him. I would be grateful for some space.'

The guy's eyes widened.

'Wow!' he said. 'Are you ...'

'Yes,' I replied. 'Eccentric, but harmless. Thanks for asking.'

He gave me the thumbs up as I left the shop. Loony Tunes blood brothers.

I'd done what I could. And I had no idea if God heard me. As far as I understood it, Blacky had to be the go-between. But somehow I felt better. Even if he couldn't understand, *I* did. And I'd meant what I'd said.

I'd stop at nothing until he was out of there.

I nearly tripped over Blacky on the pavement. He gazed up at me with those hard, pink-rimmed eyes and cocked his head to one side.

'All right, all right,' I said. 'I know. Time is running out.'

'That wasn't what I was going to say,' said Blacky. 'I was going to say that you surprise me, tosh. That for a human, you are not bad. Not bad at all.'

'Will you do something for me, then?' I asked.

'What?'

'Stop farting.' The smell was disgusting. 'Birds are falling out of trees for a radius of two hundred metres.'

'Can't you just consider me eccentric, but harmless?'

I cocked *my* head this time.

'Those farts aren't harmless,' I said.

'I'll try, boyo,' said Blacky. 'But I can't make any promises.'

The water rippled gently a few centimetres from my nose. I wouldn't exactly call the toilet bowl an old friend, but we were certainly getting to be firm acquaintances.

'Say you're sorry, Mucus,' yelled Rose.

Listen. You might think me stupid for getting caught by the old hiding-in-the-laundry-cupboard routine yet again, but in my defence I should point out...

Actually, I can't point out anything. There is no defence. I knew she was out to get me. Truth is, I simply forgot. Mind full of pygmy bearded dragons, talking dogs and harmless eccentrics. So I had unzipped, not exactly without a care in the world, but certainly with no suspicion that an alien life form hiding in a human body was about to leap out behind me and stick my head down the bog. Again.

'Say you're sorry, Mucus,' she repeated, 'and I won't flush.'

Actually, I was praying she *would* flush. This time, she'd waited until I'd peed.

'I'm sorry,' I said. She was going to flush anyway. I thought a quick guilty plea would speed things up. I was wrong.

'For what, Mucus,' she screamed. 'You're sorry for what?'

'For everything,' I said. 'For being me.'

That wasn't the right answer. She pushed my head even closer to the water. The smell was starting to make my eyes sting. Once again, my resolve to keep my dignity under torture lasted less than a thousandth of a second.

'I'm sorry I was a loser at breakfast,' I burbled, 'forcing you to make a loser sign at me, thus dropping Weet-Bix down yourself, causing you to jump and pebble-dash Dad's bald spot, and all because of me being a loser, which is absolutely not your fault.'

She flushed anyway.

I dried my hair and totted up the score for the week so far. Two dunkings, ripping me off for the iPod. I read somewhere that revenge is a dish best served cold. I didn't care if it was microwaved on high for two hours.

Rose was going to get hers.

I might be eccentric, but I'm not *always* harmless.

I couldn't believe my eyes.

The whole school, it seemed, was outside the gates. There were hundreds of kids milling around, as well as dozens of parents who'd come to drop their children off and stayed to find out what was happening. No one was going into the school. I could see teachers moving around the yard, surrounded by kids. Most were waving their arms around in a I-haven't-got-a-clue-what-is-going-on fashion. I joined the crowd.

'Wassup?' I asked David, who just happened to be the first person I bumped into.

'Something's going on,' he said, which wasn't exactly news. You didn't have to be a genius to work out that something was going on. The big question was what. 'Hey,' he continued. 'One hundred and seventy-five dollars.'

I groaned. The way things were going, he'd be offering me more for that iPod than he'd pay in a shop.

'David,' I said. 'I wish you'd offered me a sensible price in the first place. I've sold it, mate. It's gone.'

'I was negotiating,' he replied. 'You should have been patient.'

I didn't want to think about it. It would make me too depressed. Then Miss Prentice, our Principal, appeared in the yard and I put everything else out of my mind.

She was carrying one of those electric things that magnify your voice and it was clear she wasn't afraid to use it.

'Attention, please,' she said, which was unnecessary since the volume was cranked up full. There were probably people thirty kilometres away who were raised from deep sleep to full attention. 'I regret to inform you that school today is cancelled.'

She waited for the cheers to die down. This took some time. 'There is a problem with the electrics – a problem that is being worked on as we speak. But I have been told it is extremely unlikely the problem will be fixed before close of school today. Given that there is no power anywhere in the building I have no choice but to pass on the Director of Education's advice that school is closed. Would all students please report to a teacher so that we may ring home and explain the situation. Finally, I have been assured that we will be open tomorrow, so please attend as normal. Thank you.'

This was fantastic. This was just too good to be true.

It *was* too good to be true.

'Dylan,' I whispered. 'What have you done now?'

I only found him after the crowd had thinned out. He was moving among the kids, collecting money in a big tin. When I got close, he looked up, saw me and smiled.

'Explanation, please, Dyl,' I said.

'In a few,' he replied. 'I've still got some kids to see. Meet me in the park across the road.'

It didn't take long. Ten minutes, tops.

'Explanation, please, Dyl,' I said again.

'Hey,' he said. 'All in good time. First, we've got to count this up.' He knelt and tipped the tin out onto the grass at my feet. Coins rolled everywhere. Quite a few were gold. I joined him on my knees. For once, Dylan was right. An explanation could wait. I wasn't even sure I wanted to hear it. I suspected it might cause me a sleepless night or two.

Anyway, I couldn't trust him to do the counting. Otherwise, the total would come out somewhere between one dollar and forty cents and four million. Whatever, you could guarantee it wouldn't be accurate. So I started to divide the coins into piles according to value, while Dylan poured yet another cola down his throat.

'Seventy-four dollars and fifty-five cents,' I said finally. 'Plus an assortment of coins from Thailand, China and – interestingly – the Ivory Coast.'

'If I find out who put them in,' said Dylan, 'there's gonna be trouble. Still, never mind, eh? Told you I'd get money for you. Is it enough?'

'Dyl,' I replied. 'We needed sixty. We got seventy-four and a bit. Does that sound enough to you?'

He frowned in concentration, so I put him out of his misery.

'It's more than enough, mate. But what I want to know is how you got it.'

'A collection, Marc. Payments from grateful students.'

I sighed.

'Tell me, Dylan,' I said. 'Tell me how you destroyed the electrical system of an entire school and closed the place down.'

'Ah,' he said, taking another can of cola from the pocket of his jacket. 'That wasn't so difficult. Simple destruction, really. I'm good at destruction. Everyone says so.'

I waited.

That's one thing about Dylan. He has no fear. None whatsoever.

While I was talking to God at the pet shop, Dylan had been hiding in a cupboard at school. It was dark and cramped in that cupboard. And boring when he'd been in it for an hour and a half, despite the fact he could hear Mr Bauer marking Maths test papers and cursing loudly at the stupidity of those who had written them. The novelty of hearing a teacher swear quickly wears off, according to Dylan.

Most people might have worried that Mr Bauer would open the cupboard in his classroom. To put something away or take something out. Most people might have worried about having to explain what you were doing there, crammed up against old exercise books and whiteboard cleaning products. But Dylan is not most people. He has no fear.

Eventually, Mr Bauer left and Dylan emerged, blinking,

into a school that was pretty much deserted. Apart from the caretaker and assorted cleaning staff, that is.

It was Dylan's job to avoid them while making his way to the main electrical switchboard down in the basement. Dylan knew where it was. He'd spent many happy hours down there when he should have been in Remedial Maths, so the route was locked in his brain. Along with the promises he'd gathered that afternoon. Promises of money from kids who, for their various reasons, didn't want to go to school the following day.

He got to the basement without any problems, but the door to the switchboard was locked, so Dyl had to double back, nip into the caretaker's office, find the correct key hanging on the wall and retrace his steps. Not a problem for someone without fear. Eventually, he opened up the electrical mains box. Row after row of switches lay before him. And tangles of wires.

Dylan is not a whiz at Science. He is not a whiz at anything really, if you don't count window-smashing. But he had a certain fondness for electricity. Remember the scissors and the afro? And he knew that electrics and water don't mix. There wasn't any water down there in the basement. But Dylan had brought his own. After all, an hour and a half in a cupboard with nothing but five cans of cola to drink ...

Apparently, the mains box provided a brilliant fireworks display. Sparks leapt everywhere. Electricity arced. I knew more about Science than Dylan. There are termites that have a better grasp of Science than Dylan. But I didn't like to point out to him that electricity can follow water back to its source.

That he was very, very lucky he wasn't the only person present at his own personal sausage sizzle.

And that was it. Apart from getting out of the building while a puzzled caretaker raced around trying to discover why all the lights had suddenly gone out. But that was easy.

Dylan doesn't have any fear.

'Let's go and buy God,' he said.

I couldn't think of one reason why not.

The guy with the upside-down head was back. I was relieved.

Me and Dylan had whipped back to my place to collect the rest of the money and then gone straight to the shop. I'd whistled for Blacky, but he hadn't shown. Probably just as well. He wouldn't have liked being whistled. Typical, I thought. He was always hanging round like a bad smell – normally *with* a bad smell – but when you wanted him he was nowhere to be seen.

Dylan carried the tin. I kept the other two hundred tucked tightly down into my pants pocket.

'I'd like to buy the pygmy bearded dragon, please,' I said.

'No worries,' said the Beard. 'You've got a reptile licence, I take it?'

My jaw hit the floor.

'Sorry?'

'A reptile licence. You need one from Parks and Wildlife to keep a reptile.'

My tongue seemed to have become stuck to the roof of my mouth. I shook my head.

'No worries,' repeated the Beard. 'We can fax off an application form. You're thirteen years old, right?'

I shook my head again.

'Worries,' said the Beard. 'But not impossible. What you need to do, kid, is bring a parent in to sign the form. No worries then. The bearded dragon is yours.'

I walked out of the shop in a daze. So close and yet so far. I couldn't quite believe it.

'You should have said you were thirteen,' said Dylan. 'He wouldn't have known any different.'

He was right. I knew he was right. But I wasn't thinking straight. It's really annoying the way truth just seems to pop out at the worst possible moment. And now I had another barrier to get over. My parents? Signing a form to say I could keep a reptile? About as likely as Rose returning my iPod and sticking her own head down the toilet.

'How about I find a brick?' said Dylan.

I ducked into the shop again.

'I'll be right back,' I said. 'Don't sell him, will you?'

'No worries,' said the Beard.

Not for you, maybe, I thought.

'I'm glad you asked me,' said Rose. 'To be honest, I've been feeling bad about the way I treated you. Ripping you off for the iPod, sticking your head down the toilet for no good reason and generally being a horse's rear end. I would be honoured to go to the pet shop with you and sign the necessary forms.'

It didn't happen like that.

Rose got home from her school and I tackled her straightaway.

'Help you buy a lizard?' she said. Her mouth was all puckered up like a bumhole. 'A disgusting, slimy lizard? Mucus, you are a sad loser. What's more, you're clearly insane if you think I would lift a finger to help you do anything, let alone buy something revolting like that.'

'I won't be keeping him.'

'That's because you're not buying him in the first place. *Hello*?'

'Rose, please ...'

And she shut her bedroom door in my face.

I stood outside for a minute or two, thinking of how wonderful it would be to hold Rose's head down a toilet bowl. Then I went and let Dylan in the back door. It was only a quarter to four and Mum and Dad wouldn't be back from work for another hour and a half. It was time to do some serious thinking. We hadn't come this far just to give up when all we needed was a signature.

Dylan sat in a kitchen chair close to the open back door. If Rose came downstairs he could slip out. She wouldn't think twice about dobbing me in to Mum and Dad about Dylan. She'd probably dob me in about the bearded dragon as well. Just goes to show how desperate I was to ask her.

'Any ideas, Dylan?' I asked.

'Sure have,' he replied.

'It doesn't involve a brick, does it?'

His face fell. 'Might do.'

'Look, Dyl,' I said. 'We are really close here. A signature away. Why on earth would we smash a window, steal an animal, risk getting caught by the police, when all we need is to find someone over thirteen to sign a form?'

Dylan opened up a can of cola.

'It's more fun?' he suggested finally.

If there was thinking to be done, it was down to me. I should've known that all along. So I ran through a list of possibilities, while Dylan drank his cola and day-dreamed of smashed windows and police sirens. A teacher at school? No way. Too much explaining to do. An older kid? I didn't know any well enough. I even

79

thought about Mrs Bird across the road, but I knew it would take me four days to make her understand what I wanted. That really only left Mum and Dad. Maybe I should come clean, explain that Blacky was a dog that could talk to me, that he had given me a mission to rescue God, the pygmy bearded dragon, so that he could be released into the wild while there was still time to warn his family about the mine's poisoned waste dumping.

I could imagine Mum's face as she rang to book me into the loony bin.

Dylan's brick was becoming more attractive all the time.

'Get here. Now!' The voice filled my head and I jumped up, scaring Dylan who nearly spilt his cola. It took a moment or two for me to realise the source of the voice. I formed the question in my head and shouted it as loudly as I could.

'Where, Blacky?'

'The pet shop. Now.'

It took us ten minutes to get there, running all the way. And when we did arrive there was no sign of Blacky. We stood outside the shop window, scanning the streets.

'Where the hell is that hound?' I said. 'He calls us here like it's some kind of emergency and then disappears.'

'He's not the only thing to disappear,' said Dylan.

'What?'

Dylan just pointed to the window. I looked. The tank wasn't there. The tank containing God. Instead there was a hutch with a long-eared rabbit. I took a second look, though it seemed unlikely the rabbit was suddenly going to shrink, develop scales and a long thin tail. My brain tried to sort out the problem, but it wasn't up to the task. I flung open the shop door and rushed up to the Beard.

'Where's the bearded dragon?' I yelled.

'Ah,' he said, dragging a finger through the mop on his chin. 'You've just missed him, kid.'

'What?' I said. 'He's popped out for a cup of tea and a scone? Back in five?' I could feel the anger starting to gather.

'No,' said the Beard. 'Sold him. Ten minutes ago.'

'*Whaaat*?' I couldn't believe this was happening. 'But you said you wouldn't sell him. You knew I was coming back here. "No worries," you said.'

I have noticed in the past that when people are completely in the wrong, they get all nasty and try to put the blame on someone else. Normally the person who's pointed out they were wrong. This has happened to me many times with Rose. In fact, she was the person who'd drawn my attention to this fact in the first place. I remembered about a year before, she'd dropped my mobile phone down the toilet. Obviously, she had a thing about toilets. Anyway, when I'd pointed out that she had been careless with my property – property I hadn't given her permission to use – she'd got really mad.

'It's your own fault anyway, Mucus,' she'd said.

'How do you figure that?' I'd asked.

'You always leave the toilet seat up, you festering little

boil. If you didn't do that, it wouldn't have fallen in. I can't believe you can be so careless.'

The way she'd argued it, I was lucky she hadn't demanded compensation for emotional upset.

I hated Rose.

But not as much as I hated the Beard at that moment.

'Listen, kid,' he said. 'You said you'd be back. You weren't.'

'Hello?' I said, indicating my body. 'What's this, then? A hologram?'

'Oi. You need to watch your lip, kid,' he said. 'I'm sorry, all right? But you said you'd be *right* back. That was hours ago. And someone comes in with the money in the meantime. What am I supposed to do? Turn down a sale? On the off-chance you might front up? I'm running a business here.'

'You are a selfish creep. I hope your beard develops a bushfire.'

Actually, I didn't say that. Even in my anger and frustration, I realised he had a point. I should have put down a deposit. Too late now.

'Who did you sell it to?' was what I really said.

'No idea,' he said. 'Some guy. We don't ask for photo ID here. This is a pet shop.'

'But you must have asked if he had a reptile licence.'

'Yeah. He did. End of story.'

'So you saw his name on it.'

'Yeah.' The Beard was starting to get slightly irritated now. It didn't happen like this in detective stories. Put pressure on and witnesses normally coughed up valuable information. 'But I don't remember the name. Look, kid. You buying something? 'Cos if not I've got work to do. Hey, you! Stop doing that!'

It was Dylan. He'd grown bored with the conversation and had wandered off to look at some of the tanks. The reptile tanks. And, given it was Dylan we're talking about, he'd also decided to open one. The Beard rushed out from behind the counter just as Dyl grabbed a dark snake from its tank and held it up to the light. It wasn't a huge snake. About half a metre. But it was lively. Its head twisted back and forth looking for something to bite. Dylan's arm seemed a likely target.

'That's a jungle python,' screamed the Beard. 'It'll bite you.'

'It bites me, I bite it back,' said Dylan. He would too. I had no idea if the snake was poisonous, but I felt fairly sure Dylan was.

'Put it down,' yelled the Beard.

'Okay,' said Dylan, dropping the snake onto the floor where it immediately writhed under the row of tanks and disappeared into the darkness.

'Oh God,' wailed the Beard, dropping to his knees and peering into the shadows. We left the shop. I was tempted to wait a while. There was an outside chance the snake would latch on to the guy's nose. Or lose itself in his facial hair. But I was too depressed to bother. This mission had been difficult to start with. Now it was becoming impossible.

We wandered along the mall. I didn't have any idea where I was going. I even kept a lookout in case I spotted some guy sitting at an outdoor cafe with God on his lap.

The mall, however, was God-less.

But it wasn't dog-less. Blacky came running up through a crowd of pedestrians. He was panting.

'I give you a simple job,' he said. 'And you blow it. You, tosh, are a complete waste of time and space. Just my luck that of all the people in the world, you are the only one within hundreds of kilometres who can communicate with animals. What are the chances, hey? Of being an animal communicator *and* a complete dipstick at the same time?'

It seemed like everyone was having a go at me today and I wasn't in the mood.

'Yeah, well,' I replied. I think I put my hands on my hips. 'It isn't my fault he was sold before I could buy him. And I didn't ask for this job. In fact, I resign. That's it. Over. Done. Finished. Find someone else to insult.'

I tried to turn on my heel and walk away, all cool and determined. But Blacky sank his teeth into my shoe. I nearly fell. I tried to wrench my foot away, but the dog had the pulling power of a Falcon ute. I hopped a few paces, but couldn't get loose.

'Look, mush,' said Blacky. 'You *have* to do this. You can't just walk away.'

He was right there. I couldn't. It was strange gazing down at the dog's jaws clamped around my footwear and hearing his voice in my head. I wished he would move his lips when he spoke. It would give me a chance at a getaway. 'Unless,' he continued, 'you really want to be like the rest of your race. Give up. Not your problem. Good on destruction, bad on construction. It's only a dumb animal, after all. Not worth bothering with.'

'I know what you're doing,' I said. 'This is just emotional blackmail.'

'Yeah,' said Blacky. 'Is it working?'

Unfortunately, it was. I was still angry at the unfairness of it all, but I remembered those facts and figures I had looked up on the internet, the information written down in that pamphlet, and I knew I couldn't leave God to his fate. Not until I had done everything in my power to help.

'All right, all right,' I said. 'Let me go. I'll try, if for no other reason than it looks like the only way to get rid of you. You *will* go when all this is over?'

'I'm not here for your stimulating company,' said Blacky, releasing my foot. 'Get this job done and I'm outta here.'

'Promise?'

'I swear.'

'Shake on it?'

'I told you before. Put one finger near my paw and it's the last you'll see of it.'

'Why do you have to be so horrible to me?' I said.

'I don't *have* to be,' he replied. 'It's just more fun this way.'

I scratched my head.

'Okay,' I said. 'But I have no idea where God's gone. This is a big city and he could be anywhere.'

'You are forgetting one thing,' said Blacky. 'Me. While you and your sad apology for a friend here were chatting to that bushpig of a pet shop owner, I was actually getting something done. I followed the human who bought God. I know where he took him. I think it might be a very good idea if we left this place and I showed you where he's gone. Particularly since you seem to be getting quite an audience.'

It was true. I looked around and found myself the centre of a crowd. A couple of little kids were laughing. Some of the adults were, too. Others appeared worried about me. I suppose it wasn't often that they saw someone having a one-sided conversation with a dog. I felt myself blush.

'He's a listening dog,' I muttered to no one in particular.

'Yeah,' said Dylan. 'And a talking one too.'

I know Dylan only tries to help, but sometimes I wish he wouldn't.

'Oh great,' I said. 'That's all I need.'

The three of us stood outside the gates and gazed up at the building.

'Are you sure this is where he is?' I continued.

'I don't make mistakes,' said Blacky. If this dog was any more snotty he'd be a four-legged booger. 'He's in there, all right. And you have less than twenty-four hours to get him out.'

I sighed.

I'd assumed God would have been taken to a house. I had no idea how I'd get him out of a private house, mind you. Maybe just talk to the person who bought him, appeal to his better nature, offer to buy God back for the same price, maybe even fourteen dollars and fifty-five cents more. Whatever. I certainly thought I would have only one or two people to deal with.

But God was in a place with hundreds of people.

He was in a school.

Rose's school, to be precise.

I looked at the blank, deserted windows. He was behind one of those but I had no way of knowing which. And I had to get him out before the end of tomorrow. This was going to be tricky.

Not even Dylan and his brick could help me now.

The night brought me neither sleep nor answers.

So I wasn't paying attention when the conversation started over breakfast the following day. I shovelled in cereal, but my heart wasn't in it. Neither was flavour. It was like eating cardboard chunks in low-fat milk. I kept my head down.

'Are you listening, Marcus?' said Mum.

'Huh?'

'I was just saying you have to be on your best behaviour tonight.'

'Why?'

'I wish you'd pay attention, Marcus,' said Mum. 'It is the first night of the school play tonight. Remember? The play that Rose is in?'

I'd forgotten for the very good reason that this was completely forgettable news. But it was also bad news. I knew I'd have to go along and see the sad thing. There'd been loads of excitement in the family a while back when

Rose found out she'd landed a leading role in her school's drama production. Not from me, obviously. But Mum and Dad put up streamers, released a hundred snow-white doves and organised a forty-five minute fireworks extravaganza. Well, no. They didn't. But they were bursting with pride. As far as I knew, Rose couldn't act her way out of a wet paper bag, except for pulling the wool over the eyes of our doting parents, so I reckoned there had to be some other reason for her getting the part.

Like it was maybe about a young girl whose body was invaded by a green alien slime that made her do vicious things to her poor innocent younger brother. That part would have been made for Rose.

Turned out it wasn't that. According to Mum (Rose would never talk to me about it, not that I'd ever ask her) it was a love story, and Rose was the leading romantic role. I remembered pitying the poor guy who'd have to get romantic with Rose. If he did anything to annoy her, he'd find his head down the nearest dunny before he could blink.

'Do I have to go?' I said, but I already knew the answer.

'Of course you do,' said Dad. 'You must support your sister.'

I wouldn't have supported her if her legs got chopped off, but I kept that to myself.

'So we are having an early dinner and getting to the school in plenty of time. The play starts at ... seven, is it, Rose? So we will need to get there by six-thirty. Rose needs to be backstage by then.'

'Don't forget I've got a rehearsal just after school, Daddy,' said Rose. 'So I won't be back until after five. I'll just have time for a quick bite before I have to get back again.'

'Don't worry, sweetie,' said Mum. 'We'll get you there on time. Are you nervous?'

Rose smiled. Her lips parted, at least. I was reminded of two raw sausages on a chipped dinner plate, but everyone else seemed dazzled.

'A bit, Mummy,' she admitted.

'And is that because of Josh?' asked Mum. I was horrified to note that she had put on a teasing voice. I was even more horrified to see Rose blush.

'Mummy!' said Rose, her face lowered to the cereal bowl. I nearly gagged.

'Who's Josh?' asked Dad.

'The leading man in the play,' said Mum. 'The one who gets romantic with Rose's character. And, unless I'm much mistaken, the boy who Rose here has just the teeniest, weeniest crush on.'

'Mummy!' squealed Rose again. This conversation had started very badly and it was getting worse by the moment. If it continued, I'd be blowing cardboard chunks in low-fat milk across the kitchen table. So I excused myself and got my school bag together.

A small part of my mind did note, however, that although Rose squealed, she didn't deny she had the hots for this Josh guy. *Poor sod*, I thought. It's good to know that no matter how crappy your own life is, there's always someone who is worse off than you.

I had an emergency meeting with Dylan at recess.

'Come on, Dyl,' I said. 'We need a plan. And quickly.'

'Like what?'

'I don't know,' I said. 'If I knew what the plan was I wouldn't be asking you, would I?'

He opened up another can of cola. Without Dylan, some soft drink company would be forced to close in a week.

'No,' he said. 'I mean, like what sort of plan *could* we come up with? God isn't here. He's at your sister's school. We can't do anything until we get there, see what's happening. So, we'll go along when school is over and suss it out.'

I had to admit he had a point. There wasn't much else to do. That didn't mean I stopped worrying, of course. Time, as Blacky was so fond of telling me, was running out.

Rose's school finished half an hour after ours, so we were outside the gates just as the kids were leaving.

It seemed like there were thousands of them. And big! Some of these students looked like they were forty-five and professional weightlifters. I'd probably be going to this school next year and it was a scary thought. I'd feel like a turkey in a gathering of vultures. Dylan, Blacky and I kept out of the way. It would've been easy to get trampled underfoot and end up as a sticky smear on the footpath.

Blacky had insisted on coming with us. As he put it, there was a greater chance of success if someone with brains was there. I'd be *really* glad to see the back of him.

'What do we do now?' I said when the flood out of the gates had become a trickle.

'We walk in,' said Dylan.

'Maybe your mate isn't as dumb as he looks,' chipped in Blacky.

I was going to point out that that was impossible, but didn't bother. My mouth had gone dry and I was nervous. No matter how much time I'd spent thinking about the problem during lessons, I couldn't see any other way. We were going to have to steal God.

'What?' I said. 'Just wander round the school until we find him?'

'When we get close,' said Blacky, 'I'll know where he is. I can talk to him, remember? I'll keep calling. He'll answer eventually.'

I passed this on to Dylan.

'Come on, then,' he said. 'No reason to hang around.'

There wasn't, but hanging around was just what I was in the mood for. Dylan, however, moved with purpose through the school gates, Blacky trotting at his heels. There was no choice. I followed them. Even though most of the students had gone home, we still met a few as we travelled across the yard. I kept expecting them to challenge us, but it was like we were invisible. Soon we found ourselves at the main entrance.

Rose's school is a rambling place, but luckily there is only one main building. About six floors, mind you, but at least we knew that God would have to be there some-where. We skirted the reception desk. Some old woman with hair that could scour a pan and a potato for a nose

93

was talking on the phone. She didn't glance up. So far so good.

There were doors and corridors and stairways everywhere. I had no idea where to start our search.

'We'll do the ground floor first and then take each storey in turn,' said Dylan. His eyes were shining. This was action. Dylan came into his own where action was involved. I was happy for him to lead. Then I got an idea.

'Hey, Blacky,' I said. 'What are we gonna do if someone spots us? I mean, me and Dylan are just kids and they might think we're meeting a brother or sister or something. But they won't be pleased to see a dog.'

Blacky stopped and sniffed at his bum.

'Not a problem,' he said. 'I can smell people coming. And if we do run into someone, I am a master of disguise.'

I let this go. Master of disguise? I had a sudden image of the Principal coming round the corner and Blacky morphing himself into the Head of English. Or a filing cabinet. But the Principal didn't appear. In fact, we saw no one at all on the ground floor, so we took the stairs up to the first floor. Some cleaners were working there and we had to hide in an alcove at the top of the stairs until they had gone into classrooms. Then we moved quickly along the corridor. Blacky, a few paces in the lead, stopped halfway along and cocked his head to one side.

'What is it?' I said.

'He's on the next level. Directly above us,' he replied.

I was relieved and scared at the same time. Relieved that the search was nearing its end. Scared because I was now getting to the pointy end of the whole business.

'Let's do it,' I said.

We found another flight of stairs and crept up them. Luck had been on our side so far. I was praying that would continue. When we got to the top it seemed it would. The corridor was deserted. Keeping hunched over below the classroom windows, just in case there were teachers in there, we moved as fast as we dared. Blacky's nose was twitching and his short, stumpy tail was wagging. We were close.

Blacky trotted up to a closed classroom door and sniffed at the gap between door and floor. He turned his pink-rimmed eyes towards me.

'In here,' he said.

It was a Science classroom. A large sign said so. I supposed that wasn't too surprising. It was unlikely, after all, that God would be in a Maths classroom. Or even a classroom for Religious Instruction. I moved towards the door.

This classroom was different from most of the others. There were no windows onto the corridor, for one thing, and the door itself was solid. This had advantages and disadvantages. Stealing God would be easier since no one could look in and spot us doing the foul deed. But there was no way we could tell if there was already someone in there. It probably wouldn't matter, I told myself. The door was bound to be locked.

I tried the knob, fully expecting it not to turn. But the door opened. I stuck my head round. No one there. Just rows of benches with sinks and those weird gas tap things. There were posters on the walls and strange-looking

devices in the corners. Boxes with glass fronts and control panels. On the far side of the room, against windows that looked over the rest of the school, was a long bench with glass tanks ranged along its surface. And right up the front of the classroom was a brand new one.

Blacky trotted immediately to the new tank, raised himself on his hind legs, propped his front on the side of the bench, and whined. Dylan and I followed. The tank had a sign on the front. I read it.

PYGMY BEARDED DRAGON, it said in big letters. And underneath was a whole load of information about its habits. A small map of Australia, with portions highlighted in red, showed where the dragon could be found in the wild. I didn't pay it much attention. Beyond the sign, crouched in the corner behind a large rock, was God. He was perfectly still, head to one side, like he was listening to Blacky's whining. I suppose he was. Dylan and I kept our faces up against the glass.

'God thanks you,' said Blacky. 'He was beginning to think he would die in there. But no more time can be lost. We need to get him out, now.'

My hands trembled a little as I touched the lid on the top of the tank. I was so glad the mission was nearly over. But I was also scared by what I was doing. This was stealing and I had never stolen anything in my life. How could I do this?

'He doesn't belong to anyone other than himself,' said Blacky. Either he was reading my thoughts or he was reading my face and trembling hands. 'This isn't theft. This is liberation.'

I guess he was right, but it still didn't make me feel any better. My heart was beating fast. Maybe I should have got Dylan to do it. He, after all, has no fear. But I knew, like a cold certainty in my gut, that this was something I had to do myself. I had one hand on the glass handle when Blacky gave a low growl.

'Someone's coming,' he said and my heart felt like it was going to burst out of my chest. I dropped my hand to my side and spun to face the door, just as it opened. There was no time to hide. Probably no point either.

We had been caught. Not exactly red-handed.

But definitely pink-handed.

The guy in the doorway wasn't much bigger than me and his face was thin, like someone had whittled it with a sharp knife. My legs started shaking.

'Hello,' he said. 'What are you doing here?'

I tried to answer, but my brain had seized up. A low rumbling sound came from my throat, but that was it. His eyes hardened as he looked us over.

'You are not students at this school,' he added. 'What are you doing here?'

His repetition of the question crushed my faint hope he'd forget to push the point. I looked around for inspiration and noted Blacky had gone. I checked out the classroom quickly, probably in a manner that looked really guilty. That's okay. I *was* guilty. But there was no sign of him. Maybe he had adopted the disguise of a stool. Or a bell jar.

I tried to talk again, but the low rumbling was all I could manage. A thief *and* a moron. I was doing myself all sorts of favours.

'Hi, my name is Dylan. Pleased to meet you.'

Dylan stepped forward and offered his hand to the teacher. The guy shook it, but you got the impression it was an automatic response. His eyes still looked suspicious.

'Sorry we are in your classroom without permission,' continued Dylan. 'But we are here to meet Marcus's sister, Rose. Oh, sorry. This is Marcus.'

Like the teacher, I seemed to be on automatic pilot. I stepped forward and shook him by the hand. The way this was going he'd invite us back to his house for a cup of tea and a piece of chocolate cake. Just before he called the police.

'Rose is in the school play,' Dylan continued. 'And we said we'd meet her at school after her rehearsal.'

My brain was starting to clear. Dylan often surprises me. Normally in very unpleasant ways. But not this time.

'Rose Hill?' said the teacher. 'You're Rose Hill's brother?'

I nodded.

'You look like her,' he said and I resisted the urge to kick him in the nuts. I wasn't in the right position to do it, no matter how bad the insult. 'She's one of my best students. A lovely girl.'

I was used to this. Everyone loves Rose. They won't when they wake up one morning and find that green alien slime has taken over the world. No rays of sun shining from her bum then. Until that happens I have to keep the truth to myself. It's a burden being Marcus Hill sometimes.

Actually, being Marcus Hill is *always* a burden.

'But that still doesn't explain what you are doing in my classroom. The rehearsal is in the Drama Studio on the ground floor.'

I opened my mouth, doubtless to rumble at him again, but Dylan was on a roll.

'I'm so sorry,' he said. 'She told us to come to the second floor. Probably a joke. You know what a kidder she is. Anyway, we were looking for her and we couldn't help but notice the tanks in here. So we slipped in to have a peek. You have some magnificent specimens.'

Magnificent specimens? Where did Dylan drag that phrase from? He normally specialised in words with no more than four letters in them.

'Aren't they, though?' said the teacher. He was smiling now. Dylan had clearly found his weak spot. 'You like animals, then?'

'Passionate about them,' said Dylan.

Passionate?

'Any one in particular?'

'The pygmy bearded dragon. Wonderful creature.'

Creature?

'Ah, yes,' said the guy. 'Just got him. Yesterday, as a matter of fact. Isn't he great?'

'Marvellous,' said Dylan.

Marvellous?

The teacher bustled over to the tank, his suspicions apparently forgotten in his enthusiasm.

'Fascinating reptiles,' he said. 'And this one is particularly interesting. You see the markings?' I'd joined him at the tank, but I noticed Dylan hung back. 'They are quite rare

101

in a bearded dragon. I am hoping to mate him. But really, as with all the animals here, they are for my students. So they can observe their habits. I am a firm believer that students learn best by direct observation, by being hands-on with the care of animals. Don't you agree?'

I rumbled in what I hoped would be interpreted as agreement.

'Yes,' he continued. 'He's the pride of my collection.'

'You don't think he looks a little … sick?' I said. I was relieved that my voice had managed to turn up.

'Not at all. Not at all. In fine fettle. Should live for ten years at least.'

I couldn't begin to explain how I knew that God could measure his life span in days, rather than years. I didn't try.

'So you wouldn't think of selling him?' I said. It was a desperate question. But I was desperate.

'Of course not. I only just bought him. Excuse me!'

Something out of the corner of his eye must have caught his attention. The teacher turned to where Dylan was fiddling with a roll of sticky tape. He had a mass of it wrapped around his hand and arm.

'Can you stop messing with that?' the Science teacher snapped. His voice had lost that friendly tone. 'That is *my* sticky tape.'

'Oh, sorry,' said Dylan, trying to get the stuff off his hands. Finally, he managed to screw up the tangled strips and dropped them in the rubbish bin. 'I can't help myself.' He grinned sheepishly and held up his arms. 'I see sticky tape and I just have to play with it.' This was true. I had seen him do it many times before. But it kind of destroyed the good impression he'd spent so much effort creating. The teacher frowned.

'We'd better go,' said Dylan. 'We have taken up too much of your time already and we really need to find Rose.'

The guy didn't argue. I glanced at the tank and then back to Dylan. This was my last hope. If I walked out of there I knew I had failed. This panicky feeling was lodged in the pit of my stomach. It wasn't just that I would have to face Blacky's anger. I could deal with that. But I wasn't sure I could deal with my own guilt, the sense I had been given a chance to do something good and had blown it. I was useless. Maybe I should just make a grab for God and do a runner. But I knew that wouldn't work. I would have to get the lid off the tank, snatch God and get out of the door, then down two flights of stairs and out of the school. It was too much to hope that the teacher would be paralysed while I was doing all that.

'Come on,' said Dylan.

I went. But my shoulders sagged with the weight of failure. I had never felt worse in my entire life. I slunk along the deserted corridors, following Dyl. Blacky appeared on the first floor. I had no idea how he got out of the Science lab. He didn't say anything, just trotted a few paces to my right. I almost wished he would say something. Maybe I would feel better if he just told me exactly what kind of a worthless human being I was. Not that I needed reminding.

Dylan said nothing either. He got outside the school gates and sat on a bench by a bus stop. I flopped next to

103

him as he pulled out yet another can of cola and popped the ring-pull. Blacky jumped up next to me. I shrank from him a little. I thought it was entirely possible he was about to rip my throat out.

He didn't. But he did lick my hand.

'Why did you do that?' I asked in my mind. 'I have failed. God is going to die in there and it's all my fault.'

'No, it isn't,' said Blacky. 'You tried. You did your best.'

'My best wasn't good enough.'

'That's true,' he said. 'But I can't ask more of you than you do your best. God couldn't ask more of you. I tell you, tosh. I thought you were a pathetic excuse for a human being, a sad loser, a dropkick, a drongo, a moron, a gutless wonder. But you've got guts. I'll give you that.'

'But the rest is right, huh?' I said. 'The loser, dropkick stuff.'

'Pretty much,' said Blacky. 'But you're a drongo with guts.'

For some reason, I thought this was as high as praise was likely to go. I nearly smiled. I would have smiled, but the thought of God in a small tank stopped it. I put my hand on Blacky's head. When I took it off I still had all my fingers attached.

Maybe I'd miss him a little.

'Thanks, Dylan,' I said. 'You were good in there, mate. Really good. Pity I couldn't have matched you.'

'No worries, Marc,' he said. 'When the chips are down the tough get going.'

I was almost relieved to see his language skills had returned to normal.

'But that's game over,' I said. And just saying the words made me taste them. They felt dry and shrivelled on my tongue.

Dylan snorted.

'Not yet, it isn't,' he said.

'You don't get it, Dylan. God has to be out of there tonight. If he isn't, then Blacky won't have time to get him back to his family. Even now, it would be touch-and-go. Freeing him tomorrow is no use. He'd die on the journey.'

'I'm not talking about tomorrow,' replied Dylan. 'I'm talking about getting him tonight. I have a plan. Do you want to hear it?'

I did.

It was a surprising plan.

It didn't involve a brick.

And it stood a chance of working.

Mum was in a frenzy.

I wouldn't have minded that so much, but most of her frenzy was directed at me. She had ironed my best pants until I was in danger of cutting myself on the creases. She had insisted on me wearing one of those shirts that feel as if they are made from plastic sheeting. And my shoes were so highly polished I'd blind motorists if I took them out in the sun. Then she combed my hair for me! I put up with all this only because I didn't have a choice. But I was prepared to draw the line if she wanted to sprinkle talcum powder on my bum.

Dad wasn't much better. He looked as if he was dressing for a dinner date with the Pope. Mum had her very best outfit on. It was scary. We looked like religious fundamentalists about to go door-knocking.

Then Rose got back from the final rehearsal.

She was wired.

Nervousness and excitement came off her in waves. She tried to eat something that Mum had saved for

her – we had eaten earlier, so we'd all be ready on time –
but couldn't get more than a couple of mouthfuls down.
I almost felt sorry for her.

Almost.

I still couldn't get my up-close-and-personal experience
with the toilet out of my mind.

Rose didn't say anything on the journey to her school.
I had to sit in the back of the car with her, of course.
Normally, I wouldn't look at her, particularly after a large
meal. But she was muttering to herself, so I stole quick
glances. She was going through the lines of the script,
frowning in concentration. Maybe this wasn't going to be
too bad after all. Maybe, up there on stage, she'd freeze.
Her mouth would open and close like a goldfish while
she searched her small brain for her lines. Then everyone
would see what I already knew. That Rose was a fake, a
fraud, a loser.

But I didn't think about all that very much. My mind
was too focussed on Dylan's plan.

We got there way early. Rose had to be backstage at least
half an hour before curtain-up time and, given she was
so hyper, it was closer to an hour that we had to wait. Rose
hugged Mum and Dad at the entrance to the theatre.

'Oh Mummy! Daddy!' she wailed.

'Break a leg, sweetie,' said Mum.

Now that was more like it! Someone who thought like
me about Rose. Then Mum saw my puzzled expression
and explained that you couldn't say 'good luck' to an
actor since, apparently, that wouldn't bring good luck. So
you had to say 'break a leg' which *would* bring luck.

I wrestled with this in my head. The world of adults is a mystery most of the time.

'Yeah. Break *two* legs, Rose,' I said, but she just wrinkled her face at me. She knew I meant exactly what I had said.

Then there was *more* hugging and even a few tears before Rose disappeared backstage. You'd think she was going on a trek through the Himalayas for two years, rather than acting in a dumb play for an hour or so. My family is seriously weird.

'Well, what should we do now?' asked Dad, glancing at his watch. 'Fifty minutes before the show starts and I'd be willing to bet there's no bar here.'

'Well, of course not,' said Mum. 'This is a school.'

'So what shall we do?'

'You guys could go in and find the best seats,' I said. 'If you just give me my ticket, I'll join you after I've visited the bathroom.'

I said this really casually. It was a brilliant bit of acting. But it didn't work.

'I'll come with you,' said Dad. 'I could do with watering the horse myself.'

Watering the horse? Made as much sense as breaking a leg.

But that put paid to my plan. Dad and I trotted off to the boys' toilets, which were pretty smelly. At least there'd be something familiar when I moved to this school. Dad stepped up to the urinal while I went into a cubicle. One of the cubicles was occupied, but the others were free.

I sat on the toilet and waited. I could hear Dad give one

of those groaning noises of satisfaction as he apparently watered the horse. Then there was the sound of running water as he washed his hands.

'Come on, Marcus,' he called.

'You go ahead, Dad,' I replied. 'I might be some time here. Just slip my ticket under the door and I'll see you in there.'

'Don't be silly,' he replied. 'I'll wait. Anyway, your mum has the tickets. Hurry up, son.'

I sat there for about another five minutes. Maybe he would get bored and leave. But he didn't. He just whistled. So, in the end, I unlocked the door and left. There wasn't anything else I could do. But that didn't mean I had given up.

I had been given one more chance and I wasn't going to blow it.

I tried to encourage Mum and Dad to take their seats while I went for a walk, but that suggestion didn't have any legs either. I don't know if they thought I was going to be kidnapped by a year nine student or borrowed by a librarian or something, but they point-blank refused to let me go anywhere by myself. So we stood outside the doors to the theatre until it was a quarter to seven and the crowd was starting to gather. Mum and Dad nodded to a few teachers and parents.

We handed over our tickets to a girl in school uniform on the door. She was revoltingly nice and polite but I suspected that in the privacy of her own home she would stick her younger brother's head down a toilet at the drop of a hat.

My experiences have made me very mistrustful of people.

Inside the theatre, the seats were starting to fill. Mum and Dad led me to the fourth row and we settled down. Mum flicked through the program and showed Dad Rose's name at the top of the cast list. She was excited. So was Dad. Me, too. But not because I was going to watch a loser make a fool of herself. For once I had other fish to fry.

For a while there I thought my luck was completely in. We were sitting at the end of a row, just one empty seat between me and the aisle. Then Mrs Bird turned up and perched herself next to me.

'Hello, Mrs Bird,' I said.

'Hello, Sonny,' she replied. 'What are you doing here?'

This struck me as a strange question. What did she think I was doing? Practising for the one hundred metres butterfly event at the local swimming carnival?

'My sister is in the play, Mrs Bird,' I said.

'Just a touch of arthritis,' she replied. 'I'm a martyr to my knees. I'm eighty-two, you know.'

I sighed and wondered what sense she was going to make of the play. Mind you, I wondered what sense *I* was going to make of the play.

Just when I thought I'd spent most of my life so far in this school, the lights dimmed and the audience hushed. The curtains drew back and a spotlight lit up the stage. The scenery was really sad. The backdrops looked like they'd been painted by a four year old. A blind four year old. But I didn't pay that much attention to the set.

Because Rose appeared on stage. She crossed into the light and sat down on a chair by a table. She put her head into her hands.

Bet you can't remember your opening lines, I thought.

Then she started to cry. That made me feel slightly uncomfortable. I mean, this was what I had been praying for but, nonetheless, it was a little sad seeing her get so upset about having a serious memory loss in front of four hundred people. But then she talked.

She hadn't forgotten her lines after all. This was part of the play. I was amazed. Never let it be said that I have *ever* praised my sister for anything. But, though I hate to admit it, she was good. She could act. As far as I could tell, she didn't forget one line or stumble over anything.

I quickly glanced over at my mum. She was on the verge of tears, she was so proud. This was the time. The time for Plan B. I leaned towards her.

'Mum,' I whispered. 'I have to go to the toilet.'

'What do you mean, Marcus?' she whispered back. 'You've only just been.'

'I know,' I said. 'But I need to go again.'

'Oh, for God's sake. Are you feeling sick?'

'Bit of a tummy problem.'

'Well, hurry back.'

I knew Mum wouldn't challenge me too much. The more talking she did and the more questions she asked, the less time she could devote to the vision of Rose on stage. I tried to slip out of my seat, but the presence of Mrs Bird meant I was trapped. It's not that she was a big lady. She wasn't. But she had a walking stick across her legs and I couldn't get past.

'Excuse me, Mrs Bird,' I said.

'Certainly,' she said. I waited, but she didn't budge.

'I need to get out,' I whispered. There was no reply, though I waited a while. So I got into a half crouch and tried to duck under her stick. I was halfway through when she brought the stick down with a clunk on the top of my head.

'Ouch,' I whispered and fell onto my belly. At least this allowed me to crawl the rest of the way into the aisle. I was very careful not to look up. I'm not sure I could have coped with the sight of Mrs Bird's knickers.

Rubbing my head, I scurried towards the exit. The suspiciously nice girl at the door let her mask slip. She looked at me as if I was something you'd find under your shoe. Yep, definitely a toilet flusher.

Speaking of toilets, I slipped into the boys' and tapped on the closed cubicle door.

'Dylan,' I said. 'It's me.'

'Took your time,' came a muffled voice. The door opened and Dylan emerged, blinking. 'Right,' he added. 'Let's go for it.'

The inside of the cubicle was littered with empty cola cans.

'Where's Blacky?' I said.

'He's already up there. He spent some time in the toilet with me. Boy, that dog has a fart problem, hasn't he?'

I opened the door out of the toilets carefully, put my head around and checked to see if the coast was clear.

It was. Everyone was watching the play. Time was really important. I reckoned I had, at most, ten minutes before Mum would wonder where I'd gone. I wouldn't put it past her to send Dad to find me. Mind you, it would take him another ten to get past Mrs Bird.

The corridors were dark, but we knew the way. The sound of my footsteps on the stairs was loud, another disadvantage of wearing shoes that would have been more at home in the Armed Forces. Dylan was wearing sneakers, so at least he didn't sound like someone in a tap-dancing competition. But I didn't bother too much about the noise. There was no one to hear. And, anyway, this had to be done and it had to be done now.

Blacky was outside the Science lab, sniffing and whining at the dark line where door met floor. Dylan and I joined him. At the door that is. Not with the sniffing and whining.

'You sure this is going to work, Dylan?' I said.

'We're about to find out.'

He peeled a thin strip of sticky tape from the doorframe. The rest of the tape disappeared into the crack. Dylan pulled the tape firmly. Another five or six centimetres slid out. He took a deep breath, held it and pushed against the door. I was aware I was holding my breath as well. I think Blacky might have made it three of us.

The door opened.

'Piece of cake,' said Dylan.

He explained it all to me later. How, while I was talking to the Science teacher, he had been placing a strip of sticky tape into the lock mechanism, smoothing it down so no one could tell it was there unless they looked very closely. He knew the door would be locked. But Dylan knows about locks, particularly school locks. It is one of his specialities to be able to get into locked classrooms, hide in cupboards and then scare the poo out of teachers who think they are alone by leaping out and yelling like a lunatic. Doing what comes naturally.

As Dylan told it, pulling on the tape would force the wedge-shaped metal piece back into the doorframe, thus opening the door. A bit like the way burglars are supposed to be able to use credit cards to force locks. He swore it would work. And it had. I shouldn't have doubted him.

We all started breathing again and made our way over to the tanks lined up along the window. It was dark in here, but the window gave some light. This time I didn't mess around. I opened the tank and God slithered out. He was like a flash of shadow, disappearing down the side of the bench towards Blacky. I felt an amazing sense of relief.

'Good job, Dylan,' I said. I meant it, too. I could never have done this without him. 'Now let's get out of here.'

'In a minute,' he said, pulling something from his pocket and putting it into the now empty tank.

'What is that?' I asked. Even though I was in a rush to get back to the play before Mum got suspicious I put my face to the glass and peered into the gloom. Sitting in the corner of the tank was a green plastic crocodile, one of those toys you can get at the local nothing-more-than-two-dollars shop.

'It's a decoy,' said Dylan. 'I bought it on my way here.'

'Dylan,' I replied. 'That's a green plastic crocodile, mate.'

'I know,' he said. 'But I was hoping that from a distance it might look like a pygmy bearded dragon.'

'Maybe from a distance of about two hundred kilometres. But anyone closer would spot it in a instant. For one thing, it's green. For another, it's plastic. And thirdly – I hope I'm not being too picky here – it's a crocodile.'

'Well, I know it's not going to fool anyone for too long, but I just thought that maybe if the teacher was a bit short-sighted he might not notice for a day or two.'

'Dylan, he'd have to be totally blind. And he's not. Anyway, it doesn't matter, because I'm also leaving this.' I took an envelope from the inside of my jacket pocket. Yes, I was wearing a suit jacket. It doesn't get much sadder than that. Inside the envelope was two hundred and sixty dollars in cash. And a note saying sorry. The way I looked at it, I was doing the school a favour. The teacher could get a replacement, a replacement that wasn't going to cark it in a few days. No one was going to be a loser.

I propped the envelope against the glass of the tank. They might as well keep the green plastic crocodile, I thought. At least it wouldn't cost a fortune in food and you didn't need a licence.

We stepped outside the Science lab and closed the door. I tested it. Locked. Part of me was pleased at this. How would they solve the mystery of the disappearing dragon? 'The door was locked, Superintendent. Yet the thief managed to get into the lab, spirit the animal away and leave a made-in-China plastic crocodile in its place.'

Sherlock Holmes would have difficulty getting to the truth of this one.

'A quick word, tosh, before we leave.'

I squatted down at Blacky's side. I could see God on his neck, legs splayed, holding on, I imagined, for grim death.

'How are you going to get out of here?' I asked.

'Can't see that being a problem,' replied Blacky. 'I mean, it's not like they're going to lock the door to keep us in when I pad down there. A mangy dog. A smelly dog. I think they'll just open the door and be glad when I've gone.'

I couldn't fault his logic. I figured much the same would apply to Dylan's getaway.

'Good luck on the journey,' I said. 'I'll ... I'll miss you. A bit.'

'If I'm back this way, I'll drop in to say hello.'

'No more dumping on my doona.'

'Promise. I'll even shake on it.'

I smiled.

'God wants to say thank you,' said Blacky. 'He thinks it's going to be okay, that he'll get back to his family, warn them, move them. He wants you to know that you have done a good thing. And he also wants to know if there is anything he can do for you, before we head off.'

I looked at God. His hard, cold eyes were fixed on mine. I hadn't really got to know him. But somehow, as we locked eyes, I could see a mind and a world in there. A mind and a world that was very different from anything I could imagine. But as important as my own, in its way.

The world was a messed-up place and I'd only tidied a tiny, tiny part of it. But I can't tell you how good I felt about myself.

'It's funny you mention that, God,' I said. 'But there is one thing you could do for me, if you have time.'

And, pressing my mouth to the side of his scaly head, I told him.

I set fire to Mrs Bird's walking stick with a blowtorch so I could get back in to my seat.

Actually, I didn't. I crawled under her cane again. She glanced down when I was halfway through.

'Hello, Sonny,' she said. 'What are you doing here?'

'Twenty-five past seven,' I said. Two can play that game. Mum gave me a hard stare, but I kept my eyes fixed on the stage. Rose was still on it, talking to some guy with gelled hair that fell in a wave over one eye. This, I assumed, was the poor loser she had the hots for. He couldn't act to save his life. That was clear within thirty seconds. The words came out of his mouth as if he'd just learnt them, which of course he had. But there was no expression in his voice. Rose, in the meantime, was going for an Oscar. *Everything* she said had expression in it.

I had no idea what was going on. People wandered on and off the stage, talking. Boy, was there a lot of talking! But nothing seemed to be happening. Laughter.

A few tears, mainly from Rose. The occasional waving around of arms. And words. An endless stream of words.

'Isn't it good?' Mum whispered in my ear.

It wasn't. It was sad. Maybe I'm old-fashioned but I reckon stuff should happen, whether it's in a TV program or a play. A car chase. Okay, I know that's difficult on a stage. A bomb. A train crash. Even more difficult on a stage. Something. Anything. If I wanted to simply listen to people natter on, I'd pay attention in class, that's all I'm saying. After ten minutes, I'd have given anything to see Dylan up there with a brick in his hand.

So, when it happened, I think I did the audience a huge favour.

Rose was with the gelled guy. They were having a passionate conversation. I have no idea about what, since I'd given up listening at that point. There was just the two of them on stage, face to face, a spotlight picking them out. And that's when I saw him.

I doubt if anyone else did. It was just a dark flash across the stage floor, like a small shadow. It stopped at the gelled guy's foot. I held my breath.

The play was obviously set in the past because all the actors were wearing weird costumes. And plenty of them. Rose, for example, had a huge dress on. The guy had heavy trousers, a thick shirt and a padded waistcoat. It must have been like carrying around his own personal sauna. This probably explained why he didn't notice a pygmy bearded dragon climbing up his leg, scuttling across the waistcoat and settling by his collar. Rose didn't notice anything either. I suppose she was too busy putting expression into her voice. They were looking deep into each other's eyes. There was a pause. Dramatic.

Then Rose screamed and there was no mistaking the expression in *that*.

According to what she told Mum later, she couldn't help herself. One moment she was gazing adoringly into the gelled freak's eyes, the next she saw a lizard appear over the guy's left shoulder. It puffed up its beard and hissed at her. The scream came out before she knew it. Without thinking, she slapped at the lizard. Fortunately, or unfortunately according to your point of view, she missed because the reptile slithered out of sight and down the guy's back. What she didn't miss, however, was her fellow actor's face. There was a loud slap that jerked his head back.

Never in my wildest dreams could I have hoped for a result like this. And then it got better.

The guy – what was his name? Josh – slapped her back. It wasn't in the script, but then neither was getting a backhander from Rose. What should have followed was a kiss. Thank God we all missed it. I suppose Josh was taken by surprise and acted on instinct. At least it showed he *could* act.

Rose stood there for a moment, totally bewildered. Then she kneed him in the nuts. I can't tell you how brilliant it all was. Josh gave a thin scream and doubled over. The audience gasped. I suppose they thought it was all in the script. Probably thinking, 'Wow, this is realistic.' What clearly wasn't in the script, however, was a dirty-white dog bounding onto the stage, biting Josh on the leg and then running down the aisle towards the exit doors. He went past me in a flash, but I noticed a small lizard clinging to the fur on his neck. I must have been the only one who did. I craned my neck and looked behind me. The rest of the audience were doing the same. Dylan had the door open and Blacky flashed through it. There was a muffled scream – probably from the toilet-flushing girl on ticket duty – and then silence. We all turned back to the stage.

Josh didn't know whether to cradle his aching groin or attend to the bite in his leg. He just thrashed around and moaned. Rose gazed down at him with horrified eyes. Then the teachers arrived on stage. They bustled around the fallen actor. Finally one raised his head and appealed to the audience.

'Is there a doctor in the house?' he said.

A stunned silence greeted him. Then Mrs Bird broke it.

'Around a quarter to eight,' she said.

Rose said very little on the journey back. She just sat looking out of the window and sobbing occasionally. Mum and Dad didn't know what to say either, so we drove in uncomfortable silence.

I must have been the most uncomfortable of the lot of us, which was strange given that it had all gone better than I could have hoped. Not only was God out of there and, presumably, on his way home, but I had achieved the ultimate revenge on Rose for all that head-down-the-bog stuff. What I hadn't banked on was disrupting the play to such an extent that it had to be abandoned. I hadn't banked on humiliating her. Well, not to that degree. That hadn't been part of my plan.

And the further we drove, the more uncomfortable I felt.

'I'm sorry, Rose,' I whispered and I meant it.

What I wanted was for her to whisper back, to give me heaps, tell me to get stuffed, that I was a loser and a squirt. She didn't. She choked off another sob.

'Not even I can blame you for what happened back there, Marcus,' she said in a low voice dipped in pain. I looked out of the window at the darkness streaming by and bit on my knuckle. She had called me Marcus. She had called me Marcus when Mum and Dad couldn't hear.

Revenge is supposed to be sweet. So why couldn't I get rid of that nasty taste in my mouth?

Saturday morning and it was raining.

Of course it was. I stood in the middle of the goalposts, soaked right through, and watched as yet another attack swept towards me. At least there were only a couple more minutes before full-time.

I remember reading somewhere that if you had enough monkeys and enough typewriters and enough time, eventually they would write the complete works of Shakespeare. This doesn't strike me as being very useful, since the complete works of Shakespeare are ... well, *complete* already, I suppose. Lot of effort for zilch. But I guess the real point is if you wait around long enough, *everything* is bound to happen sooner or later. The reason I mention this is that my team was leading one-nil in the eighty-eighth minute.

This was a miracle.

As far as I could tell, we had only had one attack. Even then our striker mis-kicked the ball. But it took a wicked deflection and went in off the crossbar. Our entire team couldn't quite believe it. We'd never scored a goal before and didn't know what to do.

That happened in the first five minutes. After that, we didn't get out of our own half. It was so busy in our penalty area we could have done with a traffic cop to sort out the flow. Shots rained in from everywhere.

But none of them went in.

I'd like to be able to say this was because of my brilliant goalkeeping. It wasn't. It was more like monkeys, type-writers and the complete works of Shakespeare. They hit the bar, they hit the post. Constantly. I was worried the structure would collapse on my head it was taking so much pounding. True, I also made some saves but they were entirely by accident. I'd throw myself to one side – the wrong side, normally – and the ball would be deflected onto me and then to safety. A couple of times I turned away to avoid injury from a wet ball travelling at the speed of a supersonic jet and the thing would hit me on the back of the head and rebound out of the danger area.

I felt like I had gone fifteen rounds with the heavyweight boxing champion of the world.

Now there were two minutes to go. Two minutes and we would win. I could see Dad on the touchline and he kept jumping up and down. It wouldn't have surprised me to learn he'd wet his pants in excitement. Our coach was next to him and the two of them looked like they might be sharing a heart attack.

Ninety seconds.

A minute.

Then it happened. One of their strikers (let me correct that – at this time *all* of their players were strikers. Even their goalie was camped out on the penalty spot) dribbled the ball into the six-yard box. He lifted his leg to shoot. I could tell it was going to be a hard shot. Possibly one that was going to put me in hospital. But the shot never came. Because one of our defenders took the guy's legs out from underneath him. He hit the pitch in a soggy mass and the ref blew his whistle.

Penalty.

With seconds to go.

All the stuffing seemed to go out of our team. I knew why. There I was, a dwarf with no obvious goalkeeping talent and I was the only person who could get us our first win. True, we'd had incredible luck. Maybe they'd hit the bar yet again. But as I looked into the eyes of my team, I knew what they were thinking and I shared the view. After lightning has struck in the same place a hundred times, it's difficult to believe it'll strike for the hundred and first.

Their captain – a huge kid whose muscles had muscles – placed the ball on the spot and took a long run up. His muscles twitched. All of them. The other players stood outside the penalty area. It was me and him. I crouched in the centre of my goal and touched my boots. I have no idea why, but it looked professional. I even glanced from side to side as if gauging the width of the goal, and flexed my knees. The silence was deafening.

'He'll shoot to your right, maybe a metre or so off the ground. Dive just before he strikes the ball.'

I hadn't thought I would ever hear that voice again. I whipped my head around and there was Blacky, sitting at the side of the goal. He wasn't looking at me. He was looking at the penalty taker.

'Don't look at me, tosh. Look at him. Straight in his eyes. Frighten him. Shouldn't be a problem with your face.'

'Blacky,' I said. I kept the words in my head.

'Concentrate, mush. To your right, remember.'

'How do you know?'

'I've already told you. I am a student of the game.'

There was no time for anything else. The ref blew his whistle and the penalty taker ran forward, gathering speed. The ground trembled. There were earthquakes that made less rumblings than this guy. His head dipped at the last moment and his right foot swept back.

Just before his foot made contact I dived. To my right.

The ball travelled like a bullet. I was at full stretch, about a metre off the ground. My fingertips clawed at the air.

It was the faintest touch. But it was enough. The ball, destined for the bottom corner of the net, was nudged maybe half a metre. It flew past the post.

There wasn't even time for the corner. The ref blew his whistle for full-time and the next thing I knew I was buried beneath ten very soggy but very excited footballers. They all jumped on top of me. Later, I was told they were joined by my dad *and* the coach. I'm surprised I lived through it.

Finally, Dad had found his former glory.

'Tell me what happened.'

Blacky and I hadn't had time to talk. After my penalty save, Dad had taken me to a burger bar and bought me whatever I wanted. A celebration, he had said. Under normal circumstances, I would have been all for it. But I wanted – needed – to talk to Blacky. I told him as much when I finally got up from beneath the quivering mass of excited soccer players. He told me he would be waiting for me back at my place, outside my bedroom window. When we'd finally got home, I made my excuses to Dad and went to my room. I opened the window and Blacky jumped in and curled up on my doona.

He looked in a bad way. It was clear he was exhausted. And thin. I could see his ribs jutting out through his skin. His pads were raw and bleeding. I smuggled in a bowl of water from the kitchen and raided the fridge. Three-quarters of a kilo of prime steak. There would be trouble about that later, but I didn't care.

Blacky couldn't eat all of it. But he tried and he certainly got the water down. Then he slept for half an hour. When he woke I couldn't keep the questions to myself any longer.

'Did God make it?'

'He did. We did.'

And Blacky told me the full story. How the two of them had travelled through the night and all the next day. Mostly running, and walking when Blacky got too tired. Once, they managed to jump onto the back of a truck for a few hours. Finally, they came to the edge of the desert where God lived. It was another two hours in the fierce

sun, with no water and not even any shadows to shelter under. They got there at dusk.

But they got there.

And God's family was where he had left them.

Some had died, others were sick. But the rest were fit and healthy enough to follow God as he led them through the wilderness to safety. Blacky told me how they had all travelled into the night, many of the dragons clinging to his fur. Finally, they reached a point on a rocky outcrop. God dropped from Blacky's neck and looked around. If a bearded dragon could be said to smile, said Blacky, God smiled.

'Home,' he said.

All around the desert stretched. There was no sign of humans or their buildings. God looked into the night as his family made their home. Blacky stood by him. Neither moved. Finally, the dog sniffed at the reptile next to him, but he already knew.

God was dead.

I realised that tears were streaming down my cheeks.

'You shouldn't be sad,' said Blacky. 'Us animals don't look at death like you humans do. For us, it is natural. We live. We die. What is unnatural is when species die. Not individuals. Species. And the funny thing is you humans are responsible for that, yet you don't see it as important.'

'I'm sorry,' I said.

'*You* have nothing to be sorry about,' said Blacky. 'You have made a start, Marcus. You and that dropkick mate of yours. But it's only a start. Remember what I said to you before. Do the small stuff. One animal at a time. And tell other people. Tell them we must be kind to each other. While we can.'

I wanted Blacky to stay the night. He was so tired. But he wouldn't. He had places to go. Or as he put it, bums to sniff. So I opened the window and he jumped onto the sill.

'Will I ever see you again, Blacky?' I asked.

'It's possible, tosh,' he said. 'It's possible. I wouldn't bet against some other animal needing your help at some time. You are something rare in this world. You care and you are prepared to act.'

And then he was gone. I saw a dirty-white streak across the garden, a rustling in the undergrowth and then nothing. I stared until the rustling stopped. Birds sang as dusk drew in. I closed the window.

I wanted nothing more than to sleep, but I had one last thing to do.

Be kind to each other. While we can.

I knocked on Rose's door. She had barely been out of her room since the disaster at the play.

'Who is it?' she called.

'Me. Marcus.'

'Go away, Mucus, you little squirt. I am not in the mood.'

It was a relief to know she had returned to her normal, nasty self.

'I just wanted to say that I am sorry, Rose.'

And what else was I going to say? That I had a friend called Blacky, a talking dog who had taken a bearded dragon called God on a mission to mess up her play? That I had arranged it all? Sorry was all I could say.

'I know you are sorry, Mucus. You are the sorriest excuse for a human being I have ever met,' was the muffled response. 'Now clear off and leave me alone.'

I did.

Dad found me in the bathroom a few minutes later. I guess he'd come in to water his horse.

'What on earth are you doing, Marcus?' he said.

'I am shoving my own head down the toilet,' I replied. It was curious how my words echoed down there.

I had to stretch my arm until I almost dislocated it, but finally I managed.

And then I flushed.

Oi, toshes!

I hope you enjoyed this story.

Actually, that's a lie. I don't really give a flying fart whether you liked it or not. The important thing is that all the facts and figures I gave to that dropkick Marcus are true. Look them up if you don't believe me.

Saving this planet we share is all down to you guys. Adults have stuffed it up beyond recognition, but you are the next generation and must do better. You sure couldn't do any worse. So our hopes lie with you. Frankly, I'm not optimistic. I've studied young people and you strike me as a bunch of brain-dead bozos. So go ahead. Prove me wrong.

Right now, you might want to follow Marcus's lead. And I never thought I'd ever say that. Tell people what is happening. Be kind to all living things. If you aren't, I may turn up one night and bite you. Or dump on your doona. Possibly both.

Oh, by the way. What you must (NOT) do is free animals from schools, pet shops or any other place where they are held in captivity. These animals could no longer survive in the wild and you would only be condemning them to death.

And, boyos, there's too much death already.

Go on. Make a start.

I'll be watching.

Blacky

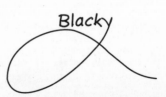

ABOUT THE AUTHOR

BARRY JONSBERG was born in Liverpool, England, and now lives in Darwin, Australia, with his wife, children and two dogs – Jai and Zac. Both hounds chewed over the original manuscript of *The Dog That Dumped On My Doona* and promptly buried it somewhere in the garden. Despite bribes, they have refused to reveal its whereabouts.

Barry has written several novels for young adults, all of which have been published to great acclaim. *The Whole Business with Kiffo and the Pitbull* was shortlisted for the CBCA Book of the Year (Older Readers) in 2005. His second book, *It's Not All About You, Calma!* won the Adelaide Festival Award for Children's Literature and was shortlisted for the CBCA Book of the Year (Older Readers) in 2006. *Dreamrider* was shortlisted for the 2007 NSW Premier's Award (Ethel Turner Award). Another novel for older readers, *Ironbark*, was published in June 2008.

All of this has convinced Barry he is a smartypants. His dogs, however, are equally convinced he is a sad loser and that the time he spends in front of a computer would be much better employed walking on the beach.